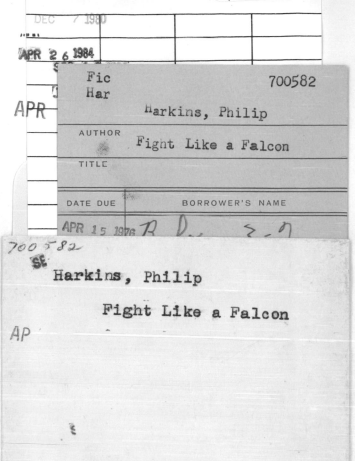

FIGHT LIKE A FALCON

By the Same Author

Published by William Morrow & Co.

BREAKAWAY BACK
THE DAY OF THE DRAG RACE
GAME, CAROL CANNING!
LIGHTNING ON ICE
PUNT FORMATION
SOUTHPAW FROM SAN FRANCISCO
YOUNG SKIN DIVER

By Other Publishers

ARMY OFFICER'S GUIDE
BLACKBURN'S HEADHUNTERS
BOMBER PILOT
CENTER ICE
COAST GUARD AHOY
DOUBLE PLAY
KNOCKOUT
ROAD RACE
SON OF THE COACH

PHILIP HARKINS

||||||||||||||||||||||||||||||||||||||||||||||||||||||||||||||||||||||||||||||||||||||||||||||

FIGHT LIKE A FALCON

||||||||||||||||||||||||||||||||||||||||||||||||||||||||||||||||||||||||||||||||||||||||||||||

WILLIAM MORROW & COMPANY

LIBRARY EDITION 1968
RESPONSIVE ENVIRONMENTS CORP.
Englewood Cliffs, N.J. 07632

Fourth Printing, August 1966

Library of Congress Catalog Card Number 61-12351

FIGHT LIKE A FALCON

"Hup-two-three!" The quarterback's bark was sharp and clear in the hot dry air that had drifted in from the California desert. "Four!" The sweat-stained ball snapped into the quarterback's hand. "Five!" The quarterback kept counting, to deceive any of the enemy who might be dazed by the heat. Then he turned, faked a hand-off to the fullback, and faded.

It was the option play. Swerving upon the scene now came the right half, Neal Davis. The quarterback turned, cocked the ball for a pass, and then at the last second tossed a lateral to Davis.

A gust of hot wind spoiled the spiral. The ball started to dip in a downdraft. Quickly Neal grabbed it, clutched its sweaty surface, secured it under his right arm, and set out on a sweep around the end.

It was the kind of play Neal liked, the kind that immediately got him into the open, where he could use to full advantage all his speed and agility. But several of the enemy were out in the open with him—three of them—the left end, the left line-backer, and the left half. Instead of running forward, Neal was forced into running sideways, and it took all his skill to avoid being trapped behind the line of scrimmage and thrown for a loss.

What Neal longed for—the smooth, swift, ground-gaining end run—turned into an exhausting scramble. Hotly pursued, he skidded on the sun-baked ground. He lurched, half fell, regained his balance, and fled. His lungs began to burn, his breath came in gasps. He was on a treadmill, running his heart out, and getting nowhere. Faking and feinting, he scuttled crabwise up to the scrimmage line and scrambled over it. Cleats clawing at the hard ground, he gained one yard standing up, two half falling, and a third plunging into what felt like an empty swimming pool. To make the shock sharper, several other players dived in on top of him. As they landed on the ball carrier, each collision crunched a little more oxygen from the small supply left in his lungs.

Grimly Neal repressed an urge to panic, to squirm, to cry out, "Hey, referee! Blow the whistle!" But experience in pile-ups had taught him that such behavior was neither sporting nor effective. The thing to do was to take your lumps, lie there quietly, and conserve what little breath was left—like a miner, trapped by a cave-in, waiting patiently for the rescuers.

In fact, with your face so close to the ground, it was wise to let it drop all the way, and rest it on this sun-burned, cleat-scarred southern California grass. Grass? These withered weeds? And as for that sun-baked mud under it—that adobe—it was a compliment to call it soil; it was about as soft as cement. Sunny southern California—bah!

A drop of perspiration rolled down Neal's nose with a tantalizing tickle. Another drop deposited a salty, tickly taste on his parched lips. The black crew cut inside his helmet was soaked in sweat. It was a crime to play football in heat like this—and on Thanksgiving Day at that!

Lying there on the bottom of the heap, Neal angrily thought of the time, many months ago, when his father's new job with an aircraft factory had forced the family to move from a cool, foggy suburb of San Francisco to this hot, dry suburb of San Diego. The failure of this end run emphasized the unfairness of the move and the unpleasant things that went with it—the exhausting heat, the unyielding soil, even the dust, just an inch from Neal's short nose.

As the weight of his opponents lifted, Neal's lungs refilled with air. He took a deep breath, inhaled a snootful of dust, and sneezed. "Ka-choo!" That settled it. He not only disliked southern California; he was allergic to it.

Wiping his nose on the sleeve of his striped jersey,

Neal watched the referee put the ball in place. The end run that had used up so much energy had gained just three yards. The same play in the cool climate of northern California would have gone for a first down at least—he was sure of it.

It was third and five on the Fairview High thirty-six-yard line. That would mean punt formation. The quarterback, Tony Spoldi, was playing it safe, kicking on third down, protecting a one-point lead. In fact, both teams were playing conservative football. The heat here in the second quarter was taking its toll. The game had turned from an offensive one to a defensive one.

Punt formation. The quarterback was waiting ten yards behind the line of scrimmage. The long pass spiraled back, the enemy ends charged, and Neal blocked—a standing block, with elbows up. The charge of the enemy end forced him back on his cleats, scuffing up puffs of dust. The enemy end was shiny with sweat and bristling with aggression. He was gritting his teeth and grunting, and his breath was hot and sour.

Neal tried to dig in and stand firm, but his cleats kept skidding on the sun-baked adobe. He felt handcuffed by the rules of the game, which restrict the use of hands on offense. Silently he pleaded with the punter. Hurry up and get off that kick, Tony. I can't hold this clown back forever.

Whump! There at last was the sound he longed to

hear, loud and clear, the good clean sound of a boot solidly applied to a hollow leather ball. Now Neal felt free to disengage himself from this obnoxious opponent, step aside, and pursue the play downfield.

At just that moment the enemy end, frustrated by Neal's block, gave him a sudden and violent shove. Normally Neal was agile enough to avoid such aggression. But his eagerness to get away had put him a little off balance, and the skiddiness of the soil did the rest. He stumbled, tripped, fell backward, and sat down with a thump.

It didn't hurt half as much as it humiliated. Neal was sore mentally and physically. He was tired of colliding with this hard ground. Each collision was a jolting reminder of his inadequacies. He had failed to make a first down; he had failed to get downfield under the punt. They were not disastrous failures, but they were galling just the same. They reinforced his opinion that it was too hot to play football, entirely too fatiguing. He was relieved when the whistle blew and he saw his alternate, Harry Wilson, coming in. Harry was a better blocker and tackler, a stronger player on defense.

As Neal trotted off the field, helmet in hand, a gust of dry wind swirled around his sweat-soaked head. It felt cool as the perspiration evaporated. It was, he thought, a little like air conditioning. Oh, if only this grill of a gridiron could be air-conditioned!

"Hi, Harry. Good luck." Briefly he greeted his alternate, who was grimly fastening his helmet as he hustled in the opposite direction.

"Fairview! Rah-Rah-Rah! Davis!"

He wasn't getting much of a cheer. In fact, only one of the three coed yell leaders called for it. But what, after all, was there to cheer about? Earlier in the game Neal had made a long run to set up a score, but the touchdown had come several plays later, when the glamour of the long gain had worn thin. Well, it was just one of those things. It was hard to be a hero at this high school. Veterans like Tony Spoldi and Captain Don Latimer were the established favorites. It was one of the hazards of moving from one place to another, especially when they were as different as southern California from northern California.

Neal made for his place on the bench beside Billy O'Dell. Billy, like Neal, was a new boy at Fairview, an easygoing southerner. His eyes were only half open, as if shuttered from the bright sun. His voice was a sleepy drawl. "Nice goin', boy."

What was nice about it? Neal wanted to say. But he curbed his tongue. Not only would it be an ungracious remark; it would also reveal his frustration, which he preferred to keep to himself. Instead he said, "Thanks," and flopped on the bench.

"Ouch!" His hands touched wood so hot it seemed

ready to burst into flame. "Gadzooks!" Instead of swearing, Neal used a word he had picked up from an historical novel he had read for senior English.

"Sort of hot, ain't it?" said Billy O'Dell.

"Sort of." Neal ignored the grammar, being indignant at the understatement. "Gadzooks." He said it again for good measure.

Slowly the shutters on Billy's eyes opened a little wider. Then he sighed, and lowered the shutters again, as if his mental store was closing for siesta time. Neal felt the same way—sleepy. He was tired. The sun was too bright for eyes to stay open. It was too hot to stay awake. Gadzooks! He must make the effort.

He had given up swearing and given up smoking—and the latter was a much more difficult abstention, in his opinion. Giving up smoking had increased his appetite, especially for sweets, and the hot summer had increased his thirst for carbonated drinks spiked with sugar. While working as a lifeguard on a sun-baked beach, he had alternated soda pop with chocolate-covered ice-cream sticks, and the result had been almost disastrous. His weight kept going up, like yards paced off by a penalizing referee—five, ten, fifteen, twenty, twenty-five. Twenty-five pounds overweight. Gadzooks!

How easily the pounds went on, how hard they came off. The fight to lose weight had started in August. By the first of September Neal had lost five pounds, and by the first of October, ten. More melted during the season, but on this hot Thanksgiving Day he was still carrying ten extra pounds up to the scrimmage line, and the unusual heat made every extra pound feel like an anchor.

He was not happy about his performance in this game. He had made one major contribution to Fairview's slim lead, but he had aspired to do much more. He had wanted to be a hero for several reasons.

First, this was his last high-school game. Secondly, his father was in the stands, which was quite a concession, because his father was not overly interested in sports. Family pride was involved. Last, but not least, there was the presence of another spectator, known as the Falcon.

The Falcon was Paul Gregson, a cadet at the Air Force Academy in Colorado, home on Thanksgiving leave. Although he had been on the scene less than twenty-four hours, the Falcon had already made quite an impression. Dropping down like the predatory bird that was the Air Force mascot, he had stirred up squeals of female admiration and squawks of male envy—and other emotions, among them ambition.

Until the appearance of Cadet Gregson, trim and straight in his Academy uniform, Neal had been fairly content with his plans for the future—to go on to

Claridge, a coed college in southern California. Now
he wasn't so sure. In the past he had occasionally considered the idea of attending the Air Force Academy.
Now he was considering it seriously. There was no
doubt about it—this guy Gregson had glamour. And
what was wrong with glamour? Nothing. Nor was
there anything wrong with the Academy football team;
the Falcons were famous. Glamour and fame—a very
strong combination.

Neal Davis yawned carefully and stretched incon-
spicuously. Gadzooks, it was hot! This bench was
like a blasted barbecue grill. And he was tired. The
heat and fatigue were conspiring, stealing up on him,
putting him to sleep. He fought them off, and forced
himself to think about the Falcon.

How did a guy go about getting into the Air Force
Academy? It seemed glamorous, but it might involve
a good deal of effort. Consider just one thing, Cadet
Gregson's build. Builds like that weren't just inherited
—they were made. Posture like that was not natural,
certainly not at Fairview High—it was acquired. And
it undoubtedly took effort. Effort, an ugly word, especially in this heat.

Neal sighed and again stretched and yawned. Sleep
was stealing up on him once more. Other elements
were conspiring with his fatigue—the sluggish tempo
of the game in this second period, the cautious strategy

of the rival quarterbacks, punting on third down, and from time to time the soft southern chant of Billy O'Dell, as soothing and soporific as a lullaby.

Thanksgiving dinner was being served—a culinary masterpiece, from the golden, crisp meat of roast turkey, to the brown crater of gravy on the snow-white volcano of mashed potatoes. And on the lower slopes of the volcano grew a bright-red vineyard of cranberry sauce. It was a sight for sore taste buds.

Hungrily Neal reached for the feast. To his dismay, the turkey turned into a football; tender meat became leather. Frustrated, he gave the football a kick. It protested verbally, and with a southern accent—a rare bird indeed. Dozing off, Neal had dreamed, and had kicked Billy O'Dell.

Neal was startled, then alarmed, as he faced the felony he had committed—dozing off on the bench during the big game! "Sorry." He mumbled an apology.

"No need of apologizin' tuh me," said Billy. "Ah'm not the coach. Fortunately for you, he's on the other end of the bench."

It was indeed fortunate, Neal agreed. It was also fortunate that the coach, Mr. Grigsby, was not a football fanatic. Of all the sports he coached at Fairview High, he showed a marked preference for baseball—an old-fashioned taste, some of the students thought. Not that he didn't like football and want a winning team, but he wasn't the kind of coach who got hot under the collar and strode up and down the side lines between frantic phone calls to his spotters, perched on top of the stadium.

Football wasn't that big a sport at Fairview. There were no phones on the bench, no spotters in the stadium. In fact, there was no stadium—just concrete stands for the home team and temporary wooden ones for the visitors. But there was a band, a little off-key; three yell leaders, two of them pretty cute; and a noisy cheering section, with the quieter spectators, like Neal's father and the Falcon, on the fringe.

Although it was true that football was not big-league at Fairview, nevertheless it was not a good idea to doze off on the bench. It was fitting and proper that you stay awake.

Therefore, Neal forced himself to stay awake and pay attention, and in the closing minutes of the first half he saw the game gradually change, by a series of punt exchanges, into a different tempo. Greenfield High was slowly but surely being forced back toward its goal line. The next time Greenfield kicked, a good punt runback by Fairview might set up another score.

|||||||||||||||||| *CHAPTER 2* ||||||||||||||||||||

"Davis!" The coach was calling.

Neal gave a start.

"Warm up!"

"Yes, sir." Warm up? He was already overheated.

"So long, Neal," drawled Billy O'Dell, "and good luck."

"Thanks," said Neal tersely. Grabbing his helmet, he mechanically started to put it on, then thought better of it. It was hot and heavy with sweat. He would warm up without it.

He crouched, straightened up, ran. He did a few knee bends and torso twists with hands on hips. In a matter of seconds the mild exertion opened his pores, and the perspiration began to roll out. Still the signal from the coach failed to come. Neal slowed the pace of his warm-up and stood on the side lines, watching. If the coach hesitated much longer the first half would be over.

Well, what did it matter? He wasn't that anxious to get back in the game. He would just as soon save what he had left for the second half. Or would he? His mind seemed to be split—half of it eager for another chance to carry the ball, the other half hesitant, content to let well enough alone.

Helmet in hand, one knee on the ground, he waited. Fairview had the ball now. Pass! The sound track of the crowd's noise crackled and rose. Incomplete! The sound faded to static.

Third down. Punt formation. Thump! Fairview kicked, and the sound rose with the ball. The punt was long, and the runback short. Greenfield was inside its own twenty-yard line.

Neal stood up and glanced at the coach, who nodded. The right moment had finally arrived. Fastening his helmet, Neal ran in at right half, replacing Harry Wilson.

Greenfield tried a line plunge and picked up a yard. Second and nine on their own sixteen. An off-side slant got two more—third and seven. Time was running out; the half was almost over. Out of the corners of his eyes Neal could see the Greenfield band assembling near the goal line. As for the football team, it was taking a long time in the huddle, apparently trying to decide whether to run the ball or kick. If they could hold onto it until the half ended, Fairview would obviously have no chance to score. But if they tried for a first down and failed, they would give Fairview a good crack at a touchdown.

Tony Spoldi, the Fairview quarterback, came over. "Play back, Neal. They're going to kick."

How do you know? Neal said—but to himself. Usually Tony knew. He was a smart quarterback and a straight-A student as well. So was Captain Don Latimer. Spoldi and Latimer—they were the standouts on this team at Fairview High. Neal envied them and admired them grudgingly—and wished that he could show them he was in their class athletically, if not academically. All these thoughts tumbled quickly in his mind, but all he said was "O.K.," as he dropped back, the last player in the one-two-one diamond defense.

Tony Spoldi was up ahead with Bob Stern, the other halfback, and in front of them was fullback Crunch Fuller. In this diamond defense it was planned that the punt would go to Neal if it was long, and to Stern or Spoldi if short. Neal hoped—at least he half hoped —that the punt would be long.

As he started back, Tony gave him one more warning. "Watch that wind, Neal. It's tricky."

"I know," said Neal, with just a touch of irritation. After all, it wasn't the first punt he had run back. No, but it was the most important one so far today. A good runback in this situation could mean a quick score and give Fairview a solid lead at the half, instead of a slim one.

All alone, last man in the diamond defense, Neal tried to appear casual, hands on hips, weight balanced on one leg. His nonchalance hid inner tension. He was worried about the hot desert wind, which blew about the field in unpredictable gusts. A punt, soaring in such a wind, could do weird aerial acrobatics. He was also worried about being the key man in this play and about his ability to perform well in such a role. It was an honor, but it was also a frightening responsibility. As a substitute on the bench he had been almost invisible. Now he was in the limelight, and in a few seconds every spectator would be watching him—especially those two who counted the most, his father and the Falcon.

Nervously he abandoned his casual pose. Moist hands dropped from hips as he scuffed backward on his cleats, fearful of being caught in the safety man's nightmare—of having the punt soar over his head. Anxiously he calculated the distance of the kick as Greenfield came out of its huddle into punt formation. The kicker was standing ten yards behind the line of scrimmage on his own eight-yard line.

A good punt in this league would carry forty yards. That would bring it up right about here, mid-field. But a sudden gust of this desert air might add or subtract five or ten yards. It was exasperating, this weather. But he must stop letting it get under his skin. He would take his stand here, between the forty-five-

and the fifty-yard lines on the Greenfield side of the gridiron.

Thud! He twitched at the sound of the lines colliding. A fearful voice inside him cried, "Get in there and block that kick!"

Whump! Boot met ball with the clear sound of a bugle calling men to battle. There was no blocking *that* kick! It was up and away, a satellite, quickly lofted into orbit. And he was the space safety man, delegated to the hazardous job of bringing it back to earth.

It was an ominously good kick, a slick spiral that minimized the resistance of the wind, until losing its speed, it dipped in a downdraft and plummeted toward earth. Neal, backing up, suddenly jerked forward. In a split second he had to decide how to play the punt —dangerously, by catching it on the fly, or conservatively, by letting it bounce.

In that split second he made up his mind and lunged forward, his big hands outstretched. It was almost a shoestring catch. At the tips of his long fingers the ball struggled like a bird to get free. Off balance he bobbled it; on balance he caught it again. The onrushing enemy ends, surprised by the bold maneuver and the subsequent acrobatics, hesitated. Neal's quick stagger turned into a low fast dash. Still holding the ball in both hands, he swept straight between the startled ends like a destroyer dodging mines.

For a second or two Neal was almost as surprised as

the enemy. He had gambled and won, and the intoxi-
cation of his victory spurred him on. Instead of being
trapped and tackled, he was in the clear, running with
the ball the way he had yearned to run. This was the
fun of football—the risk, the excitement, the rewards,
the wild cheer from the crowd, the hope of the score to
come.

He was slanting toward the side lines now, running
swiftly and smoothly, the ball cradled snugly in his
right hand. Nimbly he faked one enemy right off his
feet, and feinted another off balance. Reaching the
side lines, he danced down them with an agile artistry
that bewildered his opponents.

One yard line after another flashed by under his flying cleats as he darted deep into enemy territory.
Behind him, like ninepins in a bowling alley just after
a strike, spun and sprawled the unsuccessful tacklers.

All except one—the enemy safety man. He had
drifted with the play, using the side line as an ally and
not committing himself too soon. He knew that Neal
could run no farther to the right. One false step over
the line would take him out of bounds and stop the
play.

Neal was aware of it, too. He could feel himself
being squeezed into a trap. This trap was being set
between the thirty- and the twenty-five-yard lines,
where Neal was running at three-quarter speed. He
knew that he had already made an exceptional punt

runback, but he wanted it to be perfect—he wanted desperately to go all the way.

And he would go all the way if he could only get past this persistent safety man, who was now within striking distance on the enemy twenty-yard line. The maneuver that would get rid of him had to be carried out right now. But it had to be thought out first, with split-second thinking, as if the brain of the ball carrier were suddenly disembodied, detached from all excitement, clamor, and speed, from the sound of the hot wind whistling, the cleats pounding on the sun-baked soil, the crowd roaring.

The decision was made. He would feint lightly to the left as if to cut back and swing right. Then, shifting into high gear, he would streak straight for the goal line.

Smoothly Neal made his feint. The enemy seemed to swerve. Suddenly Neal reversed his field and went all out. This would do it. The field was clear, the end zone in sight. He was going all the way!

Was he? The persistent safety, fooled for just a second, was in hot pursuit; in fact, he was gaining. Neal couldn't believe it. He was fast, once the fastest man on the squad—once, in spring practice. No longer. He was like a handicapped race horse loaded with lead. He had run well at first, but now in the home stretch his added weight was hanging on him heavily. He strained every ligament, every muscle. The enemy kept gaining. Neal could hear him, almost feel him.

One second later he did feel him—the full force of his tackle. Neal's straight-arm struck the enemy's helmet and then bent. The straight-arm was too weak, the tackle too strong. Neal was lifted off his cleats and hurled through the air and over the side lines. Coming down, he struck the ground with a force that almost knocked the ball free.

Groggily he held on, as his momentum rolled him over and over. Finally it allowed him to stop. Looking up through eyes dazed by the collision, he saw two legs in creased trousers hurriedly retreating. A uniform, a policeman. He was being arrested for missing the touchdown.

Then Neal's brain partially cleared, and he recognized a member of the Greenfield band—a tuba player, almost hidden by the big horn. As he hastily retreated, his instrument made a flat noise, which sounded like a subdued Bronx cheer.

Insult was added to injury. Now grim as well as groggy, Neal struggled up, and took a belligerent step toward the tuba player. Then his brain completely cleared, and he stopped, realizing how rash and wrong he would have been. The "blaat" on the tuba, though appropriate from the unfriendly musician, had probably been unintentional.

Scowling, Neal turned and tossed the ball to the referee, who placed it on the Greenfield sixteen-yard line.

Tony Spoldi hustled up and thumped him on his shoulder pads. "Great runback, great!"

"Thanks," said Neal. "I should have gone all the way."

"Forget it," said Tony. "We'll get there all right, if the clock doesn't run out on us."

It was doing just that. There was dangerously little time left. In much less than a minute the half would end and, with it, any advantage held by the team with the ball. Tony Spoldi was hustling into the huddle, speeding up the play. Neal, still breathing hard from his effort, was relieved to hear fullback Fuller's number called.

It was an off-tackle slant, with Neal blocking the enemy end. The block was not thorough, and the end helped hold the gain to three yards. Second and seven for a first down. But the first down didn't matter. With time running out, it was the touchdown that was all-important.

In the huddle again, Neal could feel Tony's eyes looking him over, sizing him up. Just how much ground could this still-winded halfback gain? The quick examination split Neal's emotions again. Half of him wanted to carry the ball; the other half wondered how well his wind would let him.

"Scramble nine on three."

Relief. Disappointment. It was a pass play from Tony Spoldi to the end, Captain Don Latimer.

Tony faded and fired. Too high. Incomplete. Time perhaps for one more shot.

They hurried. It was an option play. The quarterback could wait until the last second to decide whether to throw a pass into the end zone or a lateral to Neal Davis.

This time Neal's personality was not so split. He had completely recovered his wind. He was ready, he thought. Eagerly he looked at the quarterback, pleading silently. He was still looking at him when the whistle blew and the half ended.

Coach Grigsby of Fairview was a stout, mild-mannered man. He did not believe in haranguing his team between halves. He let them rest and recover from the strain of playing in such heat. Then, calmly and quietly, he reviewed some plays on the blackboard.

Neal's body rested, but his brain kept working, nagging. It nagged him for his failure and his failings. He was convinced now that the soft summer and the extra pounds he carried had cost him a glorious touchdown. He argued against his conscience. So what? Hadn't he set up the score? Yes, he had, but he should have been ready sooner to carry the ball again. He had failed.

He consoled himself with the fact that it was the kind of failure that was hard to detect, like metal fatigue in an airplane. Neither his father nor the Falcon up there in the stands would be aware of it. They would see only the obvious—the spectacular runback of the punt. His father was not an athlete, never had been. As for the Falcon, he was athletic in other fields.

Therefore, all things being equal, why fret, why worry, why cry? His father and the Falcon had not seen him at his best, but he had been *pretty* good— that was enough. Anyway, was it so important to impress the Falcon? He, Neal, wasn't going to the Air Force Academy; he had applied to Claridge, the coed college.

The Falcon—tall, trim, erect, and smartly uniformed —represented glamour. Well, glamour wasn't everything. In fact, it could be misleading. Neal had seen pictures of the Air Force Academy in the mountains of Colorado. It looked spectacular, exciting, challenging. But such challenges could be dangerous. You had to train for them all the time, not just part of the time. You had to be ready every day, not just every week end.

How ready am I? Neal asked himself. In high school he was a B or B-plus student, with a couple of A's thrown in now and then for good measure, and he had written two articles for the school paper—short but acceptable. As for other sports, he was a good-enough swimmer to be an assistant lifeguard, and in tennis he more than held his own—even in southern California, where tennis standards were high.

Reviewing his record like this was a device Neal had learned to use when his confidence was shaken, or when he was disturbed by something domestic, like the move south from San Francisco to San Diego. It helped, this review, it helped a great deal. His record wasn't so bad. In fact, it was pretty good. There was perhaps only one thing wrong with it; he had the feeling that it could be a good deal better, if he wanted to make the effort. Did he? The question was left unanswered. The rest period was over now, and Coach Grigsby was at the blackboard diagraming plays. Neal put his personal thoughts aside and listened.

Later he stood up and cheered for the kickoff, signaling the start of the second half. Kickoffs were always exciting, even when you were watching from the bench. But after the kickoff the game bogged down again in the heat.

In the third quarter Neal got in for a few plays, but failed to make any long gains against a tight Greenfield defense. The offensive power of both teams seemed to be drained by the heat. To Neal, back on the bench again, the contest was sagging like an ice-cream cone, too long exposed to the sun—a cool, sweet vanilla cone, sprinkled with chopped peanuts that were glued on with chocolate sauce. With an effort, he jerked himself out of his daze. It was this heat, this relentless inferno.

Everything wilted under it, including time—minutes, hours. The game was getting on. It was the fourth and final quarter.

Fairview had the ball on their own forty—second and seven. Neal squinted into the sun as fullback Fuller made it third and four. Would they play it safe and kick?

The huddle broke up, and Neal sat up straight. From punt formation Tony Spoldi was throwing a pass to Don Latimer. Complete! Neal jumped up and cheered.

Latimer, taking the pass, got down to the Greenfield thirty-five-yard line. It was not only a first down, it was scoring opportunity! Eagerly Neal glanced toward the coach. Mr. Grigsby seemed preoccupied, and Neal slumped back to the bench. He was not going to be called.

But suddenly Coach Grigsby turned. "Davis!"

Heart pounding, hopes high, Neal grabbed his helmet and dashed out on the field. He was halfway to the scrimmage line before he slowed up and conserved his speed, remembering how, not so long ago, he had run out of it.

In the huddle Neal found his teammates rejuvenated by the successful pass. They hurled themselves at the enemy. Unfortunately the enemy seemed to be rejuvenated by adversity. It dug in determinedly, then charged. The thumps and thuds of the collisions were loud and painful. Both teams were acting like long-distance runners who, having paced themselves through dull stretches, were now desperately sprinting on the last lap. The blocking was rough and the tackles hard. Neal, carrying the ball, managed to get beyond the scrimmage line, but not far behind it he was hit so hard he almost dropped the ball. He gained three yards, but lost some of his enthusiasm.

It was not much fun, this kind of football, and at first Neal flinched from it. He loved the danger and excitement of broken-field play, the long run gracefully executed. It was like skillfully boxing your way to a knockout punch. But the type of football now being played was like infighting, a flurry of short, painful punches. It was rather unpleasant. But he was surprised to find himself getting a certain amount of satisfaction out of his ability to play this kind of football and to stick with it. A violent kick on his shin brought tears to his eyes. He blinked them back. The jab of an elbow brought blood from his nose. He wiped the rusty-tasting rivulet away from his sun-parched lips.

Captain Don Latimer and Tony Spoldi were whacking on backs, urging their teammates on. Go, *go!*

They went, bruised and bleeding, down to the Greenfield thirty, the twenty-five, the twenty. Tony Spoldi and Bob Stern were the blocking backs, Neal and fullback Fuller the ball carriers. There was nothing glamorous about these gains, but they were gratifying.

On a line plunge Bob Stern crumpled a tackler, but crumpled one of his own ribs as well. Out went Stern, and back into the game came blocker Harry Wilson. Grimly Neal realized the significance of this move. For better or for worse, he was in this fight to the finish.

Time out, Greenfield.

Off came helmets, down blazed the sun on heads soaked in sweat. Out from each side of the field came water buckets, paper cups, slices of orange. Neal took a slice, and with one sharp bite severed the fruit cells from the thick skin. The orange was cold, pungent, delicious, as it washed away the unpleasant taste of blood. Never had anything tasted so good, not any candy bar or ice-cream sundae. He took another slice and still another—three bites, three sips of orange juice. He felt fine, and was amazed to feel that way. Somehow he had got his second wind. He felt lighter, leaner. He was rather pleased with his performance, and surprised at his pleasure, for there was nothing spectacular or sensational about what he had done. He had simply held his own in the fierce and final minutes of a football game. He had been fully accepted by seasoned veterans like Tony Spoldi and Don Latimer. They were counting on him to do his share of a tough job. It was a satisfying feeling—perhaps a prophetic one. He had found out, somewhat to his surprise, that he had what it takes. Given that knowledge, he could do more perhaps than he thought possible.

The sharp blast of a whistle cut into his thoughts. Time in. In less than a minute or so that whistle would signal the end of the game. But before that game ended Fairview would score one more touchdown, and perhaps he, Neal Davis, would be given the honor of carrying the ball.

Line buck, Fuller, three yards. Second and seven on the seventeen. Off-tackle, Neal Davis, four yards—a good satisfying gain. Third and three on the thirteen. Greenfield was now playing a seven-man line, opening a place for a spot pass in the center slot.

Tony Spoldi threw it, and it was a little too high. It was anticipated by the enemy safety man. Coming up fast, he caught it on the run. Interception!

In a matter of seconds triumph threatened to become disaster, for the Greenfield safety man had timed his catch perfectly. He was going one way—fast, and his opponents were headed in the opposite direction. Before they could turn, it was too late. He was away, in the clear, on the far side of the field. It was one of those flukes that happen from time to time in football, when the picture is suddenly, bewilderingly, turned upside down, like a slide inverted in a projector.

Neal was still in the Fairview backfield. For a moment he was so stunned he could do nothing. For a second or so he thought it unfair that this should happen after all that hard, grinding, ground-gaining work. Despair reached for him with its clammy fingers; it was hopeless—he had done all he could. The enemy safety man was too far away, had too much of a head start.

There was a second of hesitation, a flurry of despairing thoughts. Then Neal thrust discouragement away. From inside him, out of brain and muscle nourished by the gains already made, came the strength to take off, to refuse to admit defeat, to pound downfield in pursuit. His lungs burned, his breath came in short, hot gasps, but he closed in, lunged, grasped, yanked. It was an ungraceful but wonderfully satisfying tackle—a tripping, stumbling, thumping, crunching collision, just inside the Fairview fifteen-yard line.

The whistle blew. Impatiently the frustrated enemy scrambled up. Slowly Neal got back on his cleats. He was all in. He had squeezed every last ounce of energy out of his body. His nose was bleeding again; his lungs were on fire; he ached all over.

Tony Spoldi ran up and gave Neal a sweat-stained hug. Don Latimer socked him on his shoulder pads. Neal revived. He found more air, more energy. He could go on; he must go on.

The whistle blew again. The game was over. He had saved it.

He had never felt so tired. Nor had he ever felt so well. He was slouching in the shower with the hot water hissing down, gently kneading sore muscles with a soothing hydraulic massage.

Slowly he revived in body and spirit. When the whistle had blown, ending the game, he had drawn a mental blank. Dragging himself off the field in a daze, he had been vaguely aware that he was something of a hero—half a hero perhaps. But much more important was the sense of satisfaction over his accomplishment.

This feeling of satisfaction deepened. It was a curious emotion. He hadn't scored the winning touchdown. All he had done was to hold his own in a few minutes of furious football, then to come from behind and overtake the enemy ball carrier. In the sports pages a real hero won the game with a last-minute touchdown. Judging by these standards, Neal was no hero. It was strange then that he got so much gratification out of his performance. Was it because he had doubted his own ability to play that way? Probably. Well, now that he knew that he could do it, why not do more of it? But that meant just one thing. Even in the hot shower Neal shivered as he thought of it. It meant raising his sights and aiming for the Air Force Academy.

He had flirted with this idea for some time. Now, as he became definite about it, he felt the excitement of the plan and the need to share it with someone. Billy O'Dell? Somehow Billy did not seem like the right audience. Billy was headed for the coed college of Claridge and was completely satisfied with his future. Apprised of Neal's plan, Billy would probably reckon that it was entirely too ambitious and exacting.

Therefore, Neal decided to sound out someone else whose advice might be more constructive—Coach Grigsby. The more Neal thought about it, the more logical this move seemed. Why, Mr. Grigsby might even write a letter to the authorities at the Academy saying that he recommended Neal Davis.

Coach Grigsby had a small office just off the locker room. Neal found him there behind a cluttered desk. The usually mild-mannered man with the pink cheeks and jowls was in high spirits. For the second time he complimented Neal on his play during the game, especially in the final quarter. The coach was very cordial. It was only when Neal brought up the Air Force

Academy and his chances of getting in, that Mr. Grigsby's high spirits seemed to sag somewhat. He became serious. He even made a little speech.

"Neal," he said, "I'm sure you've heard some teachers say that life is like a game."

"Yes, sir," said Neal. He wasn't sure where or when, but he had certainly heard that tired saying, that old chestnut, before.

Mr. Grigsby smiled wanly and went on. "I'm sure that you and your classmates consider it corny."

"Well—" Neal began.

The coach chuckled. "Don't worry. You're not offending me—although I used to use the statement myself." The coach moved a trophy on the desk and continued. "I got to thinking about that and added something to it. Life is like a game, sure. But what makes it tough is that they keep moving the goal posts back."

"Oh," said Neal. "Yeah, sure." They keep moving the goal posts back? Hm. It was an improvement on the old chestnut—provided he understood what the coach meant, and he wasn't sure that he did. But what did it have to do with the Air Force Academy? Mr. Grigsby was being philosophical, evasive. Neal decided to pin him down. Would he, Mr. Grigsby, be good enough to write a letter of recommendation?

"Certainly," said Mr. Grigsby. "Of course." He seemed almost eager, as if trying to show enthusiasm for a project with unlikely prospects. And the more he talked, the more Neal thought he could detect a doubt. All of Mr. Grigsby's sentences seemed to be followed by parentheses. "Yes, sir, the Falcons sure have a great football team." (But what makes you think you'll be good enough to play on it?) "There's always the problem of adjustment in such a place." (And I'm not just referring to an adjustment in climate.) "Are you really serious about this, Neal? I thought you were all set for Claridge." (And if you knew what was good for you, son, you'd stick to Claridge.)

None of these parenthetical thoughts were spoken. It was just the impression that Neal gleaned as he sat there in the coach's office. It left him with an uneasy feeling.

Neal's uneasiness still simmered in him as he sought out the Falcon later that night at the Thanksgiving dance. It wasn't hard to find the Falcon. Cadet Gregson, trim and erect, was surrounded by girls—all apparently dazzled by his dress uniform and the way he wore it. He's too conceited and spoiled, Neal thought enviously, by all those idiotic girls clucking around him like chicks greeting a fresh pan of corn.

But then Cadet Gregson spotted Neal, recognized him, and called to him with a compliment, "You played just like a Falcon in those final few minutes." Neal was pleased. But did the cadet have to qualify it with the phrase, "in those final few minutes"? He was just as bad as the coach. They were not content to leave a statement alone. They had to tack on another thought, which made it ambiguous and perhaps even slightly derogatory.

Neal was a little discouraged when he thought the compliment over, but he knew enough not to let a slight discouragement keep him from an objective. It was like football. You expected an exciting gain, and you got a disappointing yard. But if you quit, you'd had it. You had to keep trying.

Neal kept trying for two reasons. First, he wanted to find out about the Air Force Academy. Second, he wanted to find out what—if anything—was so extraordinary about the Falcon.

His hand shake was not overpowering, but it was firm. His eyes were not gray and stern; they were blue, and they had a sparkle in them. They were bright and clear, and when they looked at Neal, he got the feeling that two small headlights were shining right at him.

Close up, the Falcon was not as handsome as one might expect from the feminine attention he received. In fact, he had carrot-colored hair and a freckled face. What was it then that made him stand out—his fancy blue uniform? No, it was something else. The Falcon gave the impression that he had taken a lot of little things—erect posture, immaculate appearance, and an attention to detail in haircut, fresh shave, even fingernails—and put them together to make something extraordinary. His firm mouth spoke quickly and crisply, but could easily turn into a friendly grin. He did not take charge the way some fellows did—noisily, annoyingly—he simply gave the impression that he was in charge. He was not unappreciative of feminine attention, but he was not letting it go to his head.

Neal was impressed and a little at a loss for words. "I'd like to talk to you," he began, and stopped. That was silly.

But the Falcon didn't make a wisecrack as some guys would. He didn't say, "Well, you *are* talking to me," or even "O.K., go ahead." He waited for Neal to regain his conversational balance.

Encouraged, Neal recovered quickly. "I'd like to talk to you about the Air Force Academy," he said.

"Fine," said the Falcon.

"Shall we go somewhere and sit down?" Neal said, realizing immediately that it was an imposition to ask him now.

"How about tomorrow morning?" said the Falcon. "Say ten o'clock. You name the place, and I'll be there."

That's what I should have said, thought Neal. Now come on, think, name a place. "Sam's Slop House," he blurted out.

It was a well-known high-school hangout, but its

name could easily be ridiculed. A wise guy, thought Neal, could cut a comedy record out of my remarks here; he could really clown it up in front of these girls. But the Falcon wasn't taking advantage of the openings. He was smiling, and there was a twinkle in his eye, but his voice was polite as he repeated, "Sam's Slop House. One block from the high school on Palm Street. Right?"

"Right," said Neal. He thought, That's the first intelligent thing I've said.

"I'll be there," said the Falcon.

That was all there was to it. Conversation, thought Neal, even in the confusion of a crowded, noisy highschool dance, could be easy, if you knew how to conduct it. The Falcon had—what was the word?—poise. Perhaps they had classes in poise at the Air Force Academy. Or perhaps you just picked it up as you went along, with the neatness and the posture.

Neal sauntered away, with what he hoped was poise, and poured himself a glass of fruit punch. He wasn't really thirsty; the punch was a prop; it gave him something to do. He wasn't quite ready to dance. He wanted to sort out his thoughts about the Falcon.

Sipping his punch, he strolled out into a small garden, surrounded by a cluster of the community-center buildings—the town library, the music room, and the hall in which the dance was being held. A small but noisy group of students were horsing around in the

garden. Crunch Fuller was there, ostentatiously breaking training by smoking a cigar. So was Spike Carney,
the beachnik, a tall easygoing youth, who spent his
afternoons on a surfboard.

Crunch and Spike were putting on a parody of a
night-club act. They had acquired black derbies, which
they wore on the sides of their heads—the derbies slanting one way, the cigars another. Every line of dialogue
by this comedy team was greeted by bursts of laughter
from a small group of beachniks.

Neal smiled faintly and walked away. Crunch and
Spike certainly weren't that funny. But they usually
acted it up at any social gathering. They had no poise,
so they showed off noisily. Generally no harm was
done, but once in a while Crunch in particular would
get carried away by his own peculiar sense of humor.
Then he was apt to cross the border from comedy into
belligerence.

Neal returned to the dance floor. He was not much
of a dancer, but there was one wallflower he felt sorry
for—Deborah King. Deborah was far too glamorous
a name for this plain, thin, but pleasant girl. She
looked lost.

Neal went up to her. "Hi, Deb."

"Hi, Neal." Her eyes lit up. They were pretty eyes
when they lit up like that. Someone, a male, had
spoken to her. She looked too lonely, too eager. It was
pathetic.

"Like to dance, Deb?"

"Love to."

Neal started off all right but tripped on a turn and came down on her foot. "Oops," he said.

"Ouch," said Deborah.

"Sorry," said Neal, his face red.

"That's all right," she said bravely.

"I'm not much of a dancer," he admitted.

"You're better than most."

He accepted this as a compliment and tried a trickier step on a downbeat. It worked. The footwork reminded him somewhat of a run down the side lines of a gridiron. It was fast and tricky and had to be just right, or you went out of bounds—stepped on her foot. In one of the turns her hair came close to his face. It smelled good, but it tickled maddeningly, and Neal had a terrible longing to stop and scratch it with his right hand. Unfortunately his right hand was clasped around Debbie's thin waist. Quickly, like a ball carrier making a decision in a broken field, Neal decided on a daring strategy. Using his right hand as a launching pad, he gently spun Deborah off into space, holding her in orbit with his left hand and hastily scratching his tortured face with his freed right hand. By the time he brought her back he was in good shape again and ready to go on.

"That was neat," she said. "You've got good rhythm."

"I learned it in the backfield," he grinned. "All halfbacks have to have rhythm."

"I guess so," said Deborah. She moved her head a little closer, and Neal deftly avoided her hair—he had no desire to be tortured twice. Dancing, he decided, was sort of fun. All you had to do was to pretend it was football. The girl was the ball. Once around the floor without stepping on her foot was a first down. All the way through a set with no disgraceful accident was a touchdown.

He scored his touchdown and steered Deborah toward the punch bowl. Here, to her delight, another student asked her to dance—Oliver Jensen, a tall, gangling, bespectacled youth, whose performance in math was taking him to the hallowed halls of Cal Tech.

It just went to show, thought Neal, as he graciously surrendered his partner, that wallflowers could be put into circulation. All they needed was that first dance with a fairly presentable partner.

He sipped his punch. He was hot and thirsty but pleased with his performance. He had helped Deborah, and she had helped him by being a good sport and showing him that dancing could be fun—that is, if you could secretly think it was like a broken-field run. It was good exercise, too. He was slightly out of breath, and his muscles were aching here and there. Dancing might be a good conditioner—like road work or volleyball. Imagine that! Think of a whole football squad waltzing around a field with half a hundred Deborah Kings. Fantasia!

Neal was considering this pleasant fantasy when he heard something unpleasant—Crunch Fuller. Crunch had come inside, smoking his cigar. One of the members of the dance committee, a girl, had asked him to leave the cigar outside. Crunch had argued but obeyed, grudgingly. Now he was coming back in belligerently. Neal frowned. Who would be the object of that belligerence? Neal's frown deepened when he saw Crunch, after surveying the scene with hostile eyes, spot the glamour boy of the dance—the Falcon. There was a natural target! And here, thought Neal, comes trouble.

It came quickly. Crunch ambled into position near the punch bowl and taunted the Falcon when the cadet refilled his partner's glass. "Hey, Fly Boy! Where d'ja get that fancy suit?"

The Falcon smiled. "From a tailor," he said, and walked away.

Crunch pursued him. "Where's your plane, Fly Boy—grounded?"

The Falcon stopped and turned; his smile had gone. His carrot-colored hair seemed to have a slightly redder tinge. "Knock it off," he said.

"You mean me?" said Crunch with mock surprise.

"I mean you," said the Falcon quietly.

"Wanna come outside and repeat that?" said Crunch.

"If you insist," said the Falcon. He turned to his partner. "I'll be right back," he said.

"That's what you think," said Crunch.

The only good thing about it, thought Neal, was that the Falcon had handled it so quietly that most of the dancers, involved in their own affairs, were unaware of the incident. Neal was one of the few who followed the Falcon and Crunch Fuller into the garden.

Neal was annoyed as well as nervous. This unpleasant fight was obviously Fuller's fault. It was one thing to envy a glamour boy and quite another to let envy get the better of you, so that you taunted him into a fight. Neal hoped that the fight would be short—a knockdown or two, perhaps a bloody nose or a cut lip, and then an armistice. Neal would be glad to mediate and save the Falcon a beating, for Fuller was obviously the stronger of the two.

Neal was rehearsing his role as mediator, when the combatants suddenly squared off and Fuller charged in, fists up. Without warning, the fullback went flying through the air to land on his back with a thud that reverberated off the garden walls. Judo!

Fuller lay there for a moment gasping for breath, then staggered to his feet like a fighter trying to avoid the fatal count of ten. Gathering his stricken strength, he charged again, his right fist cocked for a haymaker.

It was his right fist, Neal noted, that was Fuller's undoing. It was this fist that the Falcon grabbed and twisted. Following it unwillingly, the fullback was turned, levered, lifted over the Falcon's crouching back, and catapulted through the air. This time Fuller landed in a rosebush, and the thorns stuck in him. Sharp yips of pain mingled with grunts and groans as the fullback slowly disentangled himself from the flowers and the thorns.

Neal decided that this was a good time to intervene. He was aided in his intervention by Spike Carney. The mediation was well-timed. Fuller let himself be led away, shaken and humiliated. He was still muttering, "It's not fair to fight that way." But not even his closest cohorts could appreciate the logic in that remark.

The quickly decided contest between the Falcon and the fullback led Neal to a good deal of reflection. He couldn't help but compare the Falcon with the fullback. There was not much doubt as to who was superior physically and mentally. But it did not necessarily follow that Academy cadets were always superior to high-school students. Players like Tony Spoldi and Don Latimer were first-class, on the field and off it.

Spoldi and Latimer were in the top ten at Fairview High, academically as well as athletically. They were headed for first-class colleges—Spoldi for the University of California at Berkeley and Latimer for Stanford. Behind them at Fairview were bunched the B and B-plus students, like Neal and Bob Stern and Harry Wilson. From time to time some member of the B's performed for a while like an A, but the effort was rarely sufficiently sustained to cause a permanent change of status.

Several questions had cropped up, which, thought Neal, urgently needed answers. Could he make the big change from B to A and make it stick? His performance in the last few minutes of the Greenfield game had shown him that he could make the A group athletically. But could he make it academically? Could he qualify for the Air Force Academy if he did decide to go there? The meeting with the Falcon in the morning should be the first step toward the answers.

CHAPTER 4

Sam's Slop House was just a joint, with a soda fountain, a short-order cook, a jukebox, and booths. It was named after its owner, Sam, who was as sloppy as his house. Sam always seemed to need a shave, a haircut, and a toothpick.

It occurred to Neal, as he approached Sam's Slop House, that it was the hangout of beachniks like Spike Carney and Crunch Fuller. It was an uneasy thought. If Crunch could stir up some of his cronies, a fight might be forthcoming. But, thought Neal, couldn't he and the judo-trained Falcon handle any troublemakers? Neal felt a tremor of apprehension. He wasn't sure—especially of himself—and he was afraid, a little. Then the Falcon came upon the scene, and the way he did it and the sight of him were reassuring.

He drove up quietly in his coupé, without making the brakes scream in protest or the engine roar in defiance. He got out, and he stood up straight, and Neal could see why he had tossed a far heavier opponent on his back. The Falcon was wearing, in this heat, not his uniform but a tennis shirt and shorts. The straight, broad lines of the shoulders were easy to see as were the well-developed muscles of the arms and legs. They did not bulge, those muscles, but they were obviously strong. They spoke softly of well-co-ordinated strength.

The Falcon's smile was friendly but not insincerely sunny, his voice rather deep but not booming. He did not briskly assume command, but neither did he give the impression that he was here just to trade small talk. His presence gave Neal a confidence that he had lacked. As they entered the high-school hangout Neal didn't care whom they would find there; he was sure that he and the Falcon could handle them.

They found no one except Sam himself, hunched over the cigar counter rubbing his gray stubble of beard. The Slop House was almost empty. Neal slid into a booth near the door and was about to sit on his spine when he noticed how the Falcon sat—straight. Neal decided to do the same. But if he orders buttermilk, thought Neal, I will not continue to follow the leader.

The Falcon ordered plain milk. This, thought Neal, I can take. "Two," he said aloud. It certainly wasn't exciting but, after all, it was better than buttermilk.

Without waiting for the drinks, the Falcon got right to the point—Neal's interest in the Air Force Academy. At the dance the Falcon had been fairly friendly. Now he was businesslike. Neal got the uneasy impression that he was taking his first exam—an oral one—in, of all places, Sam's Slop House.

The Falcon was blunt. "I know you can play football, Neal. That's fine. But how are your grades?"

Nervously Neal swallowed, and shifted in his seat. Gingerly he put his best foot forward. "I got an A in Spanish and an A minus in American history."

"Good," said the Falcon, but he did not let Neal rest on his laurels. "And your grades in other subjects?"

"B's," said Neal. "B pluses. I got a B plus in English one semester and a B in Latin and a B plus in ancient history."

"Any C's?" The Falcon was a district attorney and Neal a reluctant witness.

"One," Neal admitted. "Last year. Chemistry."

"Physics?"

"B."

"O.K., how about math? Algebra?" The Falcon wasn't wasting any time. He had taken out a pencil and was making abbreviated notes, as clear and crisp as the words he spoke. Neal winced. He didn't like to see his record go down in writing. There was too glaring a lack of A's.

"B plus," he was able to answer to algebra, and the same for plane geometry.

Neal's hands were moist, and his mouth felt a little dry. He sipped his milk. It tasted flat, heavy. He longed for a light, sweet soft drink. He longed, too, for a cigarette. Oh, to sit back on his spine, inhale deeply, and blow out a long, satisfying streamer of smoke over a sip of soft drink! That was the life. But it was gone, gone for good, if he wanted to be a Falcon.

A flicker of rebellion stirred in him. Why couldn't he relax, break training? But of course he knew why. A couple of long runs in the big game had answered that question. He could still remember the pain of burning lungs, the effort it took to carry extra weight. He sighed to himself, took another sip of milk, and forced himself to sit up straight.

How was he doing? It was hard to tell. The Falcon was one of those impassive examiners. In any case, one phase of the exam seemed to be over. What was the next phase? Vital statistics, Neal thought hopefully. Age, 18; height, 6 feet; vision, 20-20. Weight? Oh, a little too much, but it was being whittled down. No record of any crippling disease. He was ready. He would get an A on this phase or an A minus, anyway.

The Falcon was smiling, a humorless smile of transition, as he said, "How about extracurricular activities, Neal?"

Neal was taken aback. He had been all set with vital

statistics. Off balance, he had to steady himself to regain his equilibrium and remember what extracurricular meant. He was glad he knew—glad, too, that he participated in events outside the regular academic schedule. For one thing, he had contributed a couple of articles to the high-school paper.

"On what?" the Falcon asked.

"Oh, on a—uh—phase of aviation." It happened to be on gliders, and gliders didn't seem glamorous, compared to Air Force jets.

"What phase?" The Falcon was the D.A. again, digging specific evidence out of a vague witness.

"Gliders," Neal confessed.

"Gliders?" The Falcon pricked up his ears. "Good. Did you go up in one?"

Neal was so delighted to hear the word *good* that he said "Yes, sir," as if answering a public prosecutor. "Off those high cliffs," he continued rapidly, "on the beach just north of Fairview. An instructor up there has a two-seater. He charges five bucks a ride, but Billy O'Dell—that's a friend of mine—and I, talked him down to two rides for seven bucks on a slow day."

Neal jerked to a stop, chiding himself. Forget all that jazz about prices! Don't just sit here and blab. Make your answer crisp and to the point. Don't make the examiner impatient.

But this time the Falcon didn't seem to be impatient. "What was the article called?" he asked.

" 'The Sensations of Soaring.' " Neal was glad he remembered the title so clearly, although it didn't sound so hot when he said it.

"Good title," said the Falcon. His smile flickered. "We have a soaring club at the Academy," he added.

"Oh," said Neal. So that was it. Now there was a break, the first one. There was a loose ball on the field; he should scoop it up and run with it. "There's a big glider meeting down here during Christmas vacation," he said. "I could write another article on that."

"Fine," said the Falcon, and for the first time some enthusiasm slipped into his voice.

Neal was feeling better. He had another bright idea —to go on talking about gliders and show the Falcon how much he knew about them. But the bright idea got nowhere, for the Falcon had closed the file on gliders and was already on another subject. "How about a secondary sport?" he was asking.

"Secondary sport?" Neal pulled the old classroom trick of repeating the question to gain time. "Oh yes, tennis."

"Make the team?"

"Yes, sir—uh—yes. Number-four man. There were eight on the team," he added, almost apologetically.

"Good." The Falcon didn't dwell on it but went right along. "Summer job?"

"Lifeguard."

"O.K."

The Falcon's perfunctory approval made Neal wish he had worked as a ditchdigger instead of sitting in a tall chair under a beach umbrella. If only he had saved someone from drowning! But the most dramatic thing he had done was to blow his whistle to warn swimmers out of a rip tide.

The Falcon's smile flickered again. "Ever hear of the Ides of March?" he asked.

"The Ides of March." Neal stalled again as he nervously searched his memory. Let's see, that would be ancient history. The Roman calendar. The time of Caesar's assassination. He had it! "Beware the Ides of March," he blurted out.

"Exactly," said the Falcon. His smile appeared again. "Many a candidate for the Academy has been assassinated in March."

Neal took a sip of milk. It sneaked down the wrong way. He coughed. He didn't want to be assassinated —even academically.

The Falcon ignored the strangling noises. "Care to make a note of these exams?" he said.

"Uh—yeah, sure," said Neal, and thanked his lucky stars he had brought along a pencil. But he had forgotten paper. That was stupid. The Falcon came to the rescue with a small sheet, ripped neatly out his notebook.

"The key word is *March*," said the Falcon. "The exams are given in March, and the place where you'll take them will be March Field, Riverside, California. Got that?"

"Right," said Neal, trying to make his writing as neat and legible as the Falcon's.

"The first exam is the Air Force Qualifying Test, with questions on general knowledge and general math," said the Falcon. Neal wrote it down. "The second is for physical aptitude."

"Right," said Neal, and he wrote that down. That means, he thought, that the academic test would probably take place in the morning, and the physical would be held in the afternoon. But what was the Falcon saying?

"You'd better take a small suitcase with you to March Field, Neal. You'll be there the better part of three days."

"Three days!" exclaimed Neal. Gadzooks and double gadzooks!

The Falcon smiled. "While you're making out your exam calendar, put down College Boards. They come in March too."

College Boards. *Et tu Brute!* The assassination was almost certain, but Neal managed to smile and risk a slightly ironic remark. "You're sure there are no more exams?"

"Just one more," said the Falcon matter-of-factly. "The Air Force physical. You take that in May, provided your scores in the previous exams qualify you."

"Oh," said Neal, sorry that he had asked. He decided not to ask how long the Air Force physical lasted. Probably two days at least. He was beginning to feel weary, as if he had already taken a tough exam right here in the Slop House. It just went to show how remarkable the Falcon was; he could make an exam room right out of a hash house.

"Hi, Neal." Neal looked up groggily and discerned Spike Carney and a couple of beachniks scuffing by in their bare feet.

"Hi," said Neal.

The appearance of Spike and the beachniks would once have alarmed him. No longer. What would a small fight with beachniks matter if he was going to be assassinated in March? Well, he was resigned to his fate. Like Caesar, he would accept it stoically. For the present he would pick up his papers and go home.

But the Falcon was still writing. Now what? It turned out to be a sample letter to a congressman in the House of Representatives. "Honorable James Burton, House of Representatives, Washington 25, D. C. It is my wish to attend the Air Force Academy. I respectfully request that I be considered as one of your nominees. The following data is offered for your information."

Gadzooks. You not only had to pass umpteen exams, you had to get a congressional appointment!

"The data," said the Falcon, "consists of the infor-ation I have outlined—your grades, your extracurricular activities, and so forth."

Neal was still dazed. "Congressional appointment," he murmured. "I'll never get it. Think of all the guys with straight A's."

"Sure," said the Falcon. "But don't forget, Neal, a lot of those guys are going to Stanford and Cal and Cal Tech."

"Yeah," said Neal slowly. It was true. Guys like Tony Spoldi and Don Latimer and Oliver Jensen were not competing. But still—

"Each congressman," said the Falcon, "names a principal and ten alternates."

"That would make the odds eleven to one," said Neal glumly.

The Falcon grinned. "If you're low man on the totem pole, yes. But you may be second or third alternate. I was first alternate. The principal passed, but the Academy had a vacancy and accepted me as a qualified alternate."

"Oh," said Neal. It was all he could manage.

"Any more questions?" asked the Falcon, smiling again.

Neal shook his head. "No, no more questions." It was all down on paper, an outline of all the events. The Falcon was very efficient—too efficient.

Evidently the interview was over, because the Falcon was glancing at his wrist watch. They got up, Neal groggily, like a beaten boxer staggering out of his corner to hear the decision against him.

From outside came a belligerent blast from the twin pipes of a hot rod and the sharp squeal of protesting tires. Then into the Slop House barged Crunch Fuller.

Neal was still so confused and dismayed by the Falcon's outline that the danger of this meeting did not completely penetrate, and it was over before he became fully aware of it. Crunch Fuller spotted the Falcon, and all at once much of the wind seemed to come out of his sails. He walked by quickly, silently. And Neal noticed that he was not greeted as a conquering hero by Spike Carney and the beachniks. Apparently fullback Fuller had left a good deal of his prestige in the rosebush.

Cadet Gregson departed, and Neal was left alone in front of the Slop House. He was still befuddled by the rush of events, and for a minute or so he did not realize that the weather had radically changed, as it often did in this seaside town in southern California. The hot air from the desert, drifting out over the Pacific, had collided with cold air from the ocean, creating a heavy mist. It matched Neal's mood. He was now groping through a physical as well as a mental fog.

Beware the Ides of March. March Field, the Air Force Center. March—the way you did in the cadet wing.

Glumly he slouched through the fog. He wouldn't qualify as a candidate. He knew it, Coach Grigsby knew it, and so did the Falcon. There wasn't enough time. Why, December was only a week away, and after that there were only two months in which to prepare, to get ready for all those examinations.

Head down, hands in pockets, Neal turned a fog-bound corner, slumped down another street, and found himself on the beach, staring out to sea. An ocean swell rolled in, curled over, and crunched into white surf. Sea gulls wheeled and squawked. A pelican glided along a breaking wave, searching for fish in the translucent water. Without warning, down through the fog came an eerie whine. Distant at first, it grew quickly closer, louder. Suddenly it thundered over-head and just as suddenly echoed away over the ocean —an Air Force jet "scrambling" from a nearby field.

The shock of the noise shook Neal like a starter's gun. He began to run along the beach. It was high tide, and footing in the soft sand was uncertain, re-quiring more effort. He welcomed it. "Beach work" could be better than road work. It could take off weight, toughen muscles, harden lungs, and clear the head.

Odds that had seemed hopelessly long in the Slop House—eleven to one—narrowed to five to one, three to one, as he ran along the beach. Many of the subjects mentioned by the Falcon had been mastered, more or less. He could bone up on the B's, push them up to B pluses, A minuses, or even A's. He was in good shape physically, except for a little excess weight. He could take that off and stay in shape by beach work and by playing his secondary sport, tennis.

He jogged about a mile in the soft sand, without gasping for air or having his lungs burn. He turned off the beach and trotted two blocks to the weather-beaten shingle house his father had rented. Briefly he greeted his mother and his kid sister Karen in the kitchen. Then up the back stairs, two at a time, he went, to the reassuring disorder of his room—a sweater here, sneakers there, books all over the place. Assembling these books, he went to work on them.

CHAPTER 5

Oomph—poomph. Oomph—poomph. Up—down. Up
—down.

Neal was doing push ups. His lungs worked like
bellows, his shoulders ached, and his forearms strained,
as the push ups became harder and harder. It was dull,
tough work. There were no bands, no cheering sec-
tions here—not even the company of teammates. He
was all alone in his room.

Whump! He came down hard on the bedroom floor.

"What on earth is going on up there?" It was his
mother, calling up the back stairs.

"Push ups," said Neal breathlessly.

"Good heavens, Neal! Couldn't you do all that in
the high-school gym?"

He got up, welcoming the interruption. "Sometimes I do, Mom, but half the time the gym is taken
by basketball teams."

"That's too bad," said his mother. "But you're playing tennis, you're running on the beach, you're dieting, cutting out sweets, and eating a lot of proteins. Just how much of this fantastic physical conditioning do you need, Neal?"

Neal chuckled. "Every bit I can get," he said.

His mother returned to her chores in the kitchen, abandoning the argument. But Neal had an argument of his own. Occasionally in the past he had noticed a split in his personality. Half of him would want to go to the soda fountain for a sundae, the other half to the gym and a sweat suit. The split seemed wider than ever these days, as the side in favor of rigorous physical conditioning asserted its superiority, and the other side, becoming more irritable, goaded and criticized.

Oh no! cried his alter ego, as he reached for the "torso builder," a simple contrivance, with two steel grips for the hands and six strong rubber bands. As the hands pulled outward, stretching the arms and straining the shoulders, the rubber bands resisted. At first, three of the bands had put up sufficient resistance to give strenuous exercise. Gradually he had worked it up to four, five, and now six. As he toiled, a small fire seemed to start in his shoulders and spread up through his neck and over his face. He burned. His alter ego sneered, "And you paid good money out of your savings for this instrument of torture! How crazy can you get!"

He ignored the alter ego, put on a sweat suit, picked up a rubber ball in his left hand and, squeezing, thumped downstairs. The rubber ball was a new device to strengthen his left wrist, the same left wrist that had caved in on the gridiron when acting as a straight-arm.

His mother gave him a searching look as he passed through the kitchen. She noted the sweat suit, the sneakers, and the rubber ball he was squeezing. "What on earth are you doing that for?"

"To strengthen my left wrist," he said seriously.

His mother had been mixing something in a bowl. She put the big spoon down and said, "Neal, are you sure you're all right?"

He grinned. "Feeling a little better every day," he said.

"You're sure?" she said. "Wouldn't you like to sit down and relax? I'll fix you a good cup of hot cocoa."

He grinned again. That was his mother's solution for most problems at this time of the year—"a good cup of hot cocoa." In summer it would be "a nice cool glass of lemonade."

"I'd like some cocoa, Mom, but I'll have to pass it up. It's fattening."

"Fattening!" she cried. "I declare. You're not an ounce overweight."

"But I was," he said, "and I don't want to be again. Don't worry, Mom. Everything's under control." He gave her an affectionate pat on the back and then left, squeezing the rubber ball in his left hand.

"I declare!" he heard her say again as the door closed behind him.

The sand on the beach was packed down hard by the receding tide. This made beach work easier, so he added more distance to his run. He could run faster and farther now without slowing down to a jog.

When he returned home his mother was waiting for him with a cup of beef broth. "Now don't try to tell me *this* is fattening," she said. "Just sit there and drink it."

He smiled and sat down. "O.K., Mom, you win. Thanks."

"How do you feel?" she asked anxiously.

He sipped. "Never felt better."

She smiled. "At the Air Force Academy," she said, "do the cadets have to be very neat?"

"You bet," said Neal.

"I see," she said. "Then you'd better start straightening up your room every day. It's pretty much of a mess."

He grinned, but ruefully. "O.K., Mom. I guess I asked for it."

"Yes," she said, "you did. And you might as well wash out that cup. I'm sure they don't tolerate dirty dishes at the Academy."

"All right," he said, and then added, "humph. A

course in housekeeping. I never thought of that."

"What boy would?" she said.

As he climbed the stairs he realized that he had been challenged for the third time. Coach Grigsby had seemed to doubt that he could qualify as a football player. The Falcon had questioned his academic record, and now his mother had remarked on his neatness —or lack of it. He knew he was neat, personally. He kept his clothes clean, his hair trimmed, his face shaven. But what about this room—shoes here, slacks there, tennis racket on the bed, books all over the place? That would never pass inspection at the Academy. He must tidy it up. But first he would shower.

The shower refreshed him. He returned to his room with extra energy. Putting his books in place, he saw a memo for a date—not with a girl, because he had no time for that now—but with Mr. Sandler, his student adviser. There, thought Neal, comes challenge number four, for Mr. Sandler had already approved of his decision to go to Claridge College.

"So you've switched goals, Neal." Mr. Sandler was shuffling some papers on his desk. He was a bespectacled, bald-headed English teacher with a round and ruddy face.

"Yes, sir," said Neal. He sat there waiting for the fourth challenge. Perhaps he should precipitate it. Why sit back and wait for it? "How about my chances,

Mr. Sandler?" he blurted out. "Do you think they're any good?"

Mr. Sandler smiled and shrugged his shoulders. "I could say this, Neal. I could say your chances are as good as you make them. But what would you think of that? You'd think it was one of those pseudo-wise sayings that some teachers like to make." Mr. Sandler smiled and said, "I'll say this instead. The Air Force Academy is a new college. Although it stresses science it has a great respect for the humanities as well—history, English, foreign languages."

Mr. Sandler took off his glasses and swung them like a pendulum. "If the Academy was just an engineering school, Neal, I'd advise against your going there. You're not going to be an engineer any more than you're going to be a nuclear physicist."

"Yes, sir," said Neal. He was sitting up straight, straining to get the shading on every syllable.

"Another thing," said Mr. Sandler. "You're an athlete. You like sports, and your record shows that you're good at them—especially football and tennis. The Air Force Academy likes athletes."

"Yes, sir," said Neal. He felt a little encouraged.

Mr. Sandler swung his glasses and smiled again. "There's something else, too, Neal. We have straight-A students here, as you know—boys like Latimer, Spoldi, and Jensen. They're going to colleges like Cal and Stanford, so you won't be competing against them.

Nevertheless, the competition will be tough. And here's
something you might remember—"

"What's that, sir?"

"There are certain students, Neal—and you may be
one of them—who find themselves a little later than
others. Some boys get straight A's as high-school freshmen. Others go along in the average way and suddenly,
as seniors, or perhaps as college students, develop a
desire and an ability to be well above average. We can
give these boys all the tests in the world as undergrad-
uates, but that intangible something, which allows
them to take off later, seems to lie latent. It doesn't
show in those tests. But all at once it's there—perhaps
other things bring it out." Mr. Sandler smiled. "In
spite of all we've learned about human behavior, there
are still mysterious intangibles."

"Yes, sir," said Neal. He had expected a challenge
at Mr. Sandler's desk. He had received encouragement
instead, and he was grateful.

"Now let's be practical instead of theoretical, Neal.
Do you happen to know when those Academy cadets
get up in the morning?"

"No, sir."

"I thought not," said Mr. Sandler with a smile.
"They get up, Neal, at 5:55 A.M."

"Gadzooks!" said Neal. "Five-fifty-five!"

"Exactly," said Mr. Sandler. "Changed your mind
about going there?"

"No, sir."

"All right. Take that early rising hour, which you will have to get used to, and start putting it to your advantage right now."

"Right now, sir?" said Neal. He was already considering how lucky he was, as a high-school student, not to have to get up before seven or seven-thirty.

"Right now," said Mr. Sandler. "Tomorrow morning. Set your alarm for 5:55, if your family can stand it. Fix yourself a cup of coffee or tea, and then put in an extra hour of study on one of your weaker subjects."

"Oh," said Neal, repelled by the idea. Extra physical education in the afternoon was O.K., but extra mental effort at 6 A.M.—gadzooks!

"You'll be killing two birds with one stone," Mr. Sandler was saying. "You'll be strengthening a weaker subject for the exams, and you'll also be preparing yourself for that early rising hour at the Academy—if you gain admittance."

Killing two birds with one stone? thought Neal. Let's make it three. I'm the third one.

Mr. Sandler was talking on about the rest of Neal's study plan—study periods in school, a study period after exercise in the afternoon, study hours after dinner. "Tackle the new when the brain is fresh," Mr. Sandler was saying. "Do the review later."

It all made sense, thought Neal, and he was willing to try it. But what struck him was the irony of the interview. He had come to it prepared for a different attitude. He had expected Mr. Sandler to suggest, tactfully perhaps, that the odds were too long against Neal's being accepted by the Academy. What had happened was just the opposite. Mr. Sandler had warmed to the project like the manager of a prize fighter, with the rising hope of a victory in the ring. Your opponent is a sucker for a left hook, he seemed to be saying. All y'gotta do, kid, is to get in there and train the right way.

Neal had expected a challenge. What he had received was a new training program, which balanced mental effort with physical conditioning. To do push ups and beach work, to play tennis hard and well—all that took a certain amount of self-discipline. But to set the alarm for 5:55 A.M., to hear it go off at that depressing hour, and to get up and do an hour's study before breakfast—that took—well, it took guts—yes, mental guts. Gadzooks!

Painfully the new program was put into effect, the alarm set. BRRING! Oh, that sickening sound at 5:55 A.M.! Turn it off! Throw it out the window! No, get up. Brr, it's cold, even in southern California, at such an early hour. So what? Put on your bathrobe, stumble downstairs, and fix yourself a hot drink. Sip it. Feel better? A little. Sip some more. Drain the cup.

Now get down to work. Physics this morning. Nothing like studying physics from 6 to 7 A.M. Five minutes go by, ten, half an hour. The work is getting done. It *is* quiet, isn't it? No kid sister striving for her place in the sun, no mother worrying, no father asking parental questions.

Mr. Sandler's system was unpleasant to begin with but, once started, was surprisingly satisfying.

CHAPTER 6

In his letter to Congressman Burton, Neal had listed tennis as one of the sports he played for his high school. At this time of year in southern California, with football ended, tennis became a full-fledged sport.

The coach of the tennis team was a short but wiry science teacher named Levin. Mr. Levin improved Neal's strokes with a few reminders—"Move your feet!" "Get your racket back!" "Keep your eye on the ball!" —and improved his stamina with scientific advice.

Sugar, Mr. Levin pointed out, was not always a friend of the athlete. If taken at the beginning of a contest in the form of a soft drink or candy bar, it dramatically raised the blood-sugar level and sent the athlete soaring in a burst of false energy. But this backfired by setting off an increased supply of insulin in the body. Without warning, the insulin would abruptly lower the blood sugar, leaving the athlete weak and dizzy. Soft drinks were not only fattening, they were debilitating.

In the quarter-finals of the Christmas tennis tournament Neal came up against an old rival from the previous summer, a maddeningly methodical strategist named Wentworth Dillon. Wentworth was what is known in tennis as "a dinker." He "dinked" every ball, pushed it back, chopped it back, lobbed it back—but got it back.

In a summer tournament Neal had played an arduous match against Wentworth. It had been a hot day, and Neal had sipped a soft drink as he stormed through the first set, rushing the net and clobbering the dinks. In the second set Neal had led, 7-6, and needed only one game to win. But he had run so much after drop shots and lobs that he was at the end of his rope. He became weak and dizzy as his blood sugar dropped. He got a cramp in his right hand and a Charley horse in his left leg. As Neal reached the point of exhaustion, Wentworth Dillon dinked to victory, sucking on an orange, adjusting his sun visor, and wiping perspiration off his dark glasses—doing all these things with calm and deliberate movements that almost drove Neal out of his mind.

Now, in December, Neal came to the court physically fit, stronger, leaner, and smarter—he was not depending on sugar for quick energy. He won the first set easily and took a lead in the second. Then the dinks began to slow him up. He was running his heart out after drop shots and lobs, and the effort began to take its toll.

Sweating freely and breathing hard between points, Neal lost two games in a row, and Wentworth Dillon looked pleased with himself as they changed courts and paused by the umpire's chair. Methodically Wentworth again consumed half an orange, adjusted his sun visor, and wiped off his dark glasses. It was all part of his strategy; his opponent was supposed to be "psyched out" by these maddeningly deliberate movements.

But Neal was not "psyched out"; he had found his second wind. When play was resumed he was able to renew his attack and win point after point. Wentworth was astonished; he had expected Neal to crumple. Wentworth was annoyed. He tried to stall, but that didn't work. He despaired, and came apart as his dinks began dropping into the net. Neal's subsequent victory was surprisingly satisfactory.

In the semifinals of the same tournament he played Tommy Melton, who played an attacking game so well that he had always beaten Neal. In this match Tommy won the first set, and Neal the second. The third set went into extra innings—5-all, 6-all, 7-all. Still hitting his serve hard and following it to the net, Neal went ahead, 8-7. When Tommy, obviously tiring, softened his serve and followed it less quickly to the net, Neal broke through and won the match. He knew why. He had won, not because of superior strokes, but because of superior stamina.

He lost the finals, but the winner was a ranking player with a long tournament record. All in all, Neal could be pleased with his performance. Never before had he got to the finals, let alone the semis, of a southern California tennis tournament.

He was also pleased by something else during the Christmas vacation—a present in the form of a letter from Congressman Burton. The congressman, after studying Neal's record, appointed him third alternate. This meant that three candidates, the principal and the first and second alternates, had priority over Neal. That no longer discouraged him. He figured that he had reduced the odds from eleven to one to four to one. Moreover, there was always the chance that one of the candidates ahead of him might fail the physical or the academic exam, reducing the odds even further. Then he would be within striking distance. But he did not let himself think about this often.

In previous years Neal had always considered Christmas vacation a loafing period. In this vacation he kept plugging mentally as well as physically, and when school reopened in January his grades began to reflect the extra effort.

The Ides of March approached. Nervously Neal packed a small bag and set out for the Air Force center.

He was as ready as three months of rigorous training could make him. But was he ready enough? Had he started too late?

Tensely he took his first academic test. General knowledge, they called it. That could mean almost anything—foreign fields, foreign faces. His heart beat fast, his fingers grew moist. And then to his great relief he found familiar fields and faces. Why was 1066 an important date? It meant the Battle of Hastings and the Norman Conquest of England. Who was considered the George Washington of South America? Simon Bolívar. Who discovered radium? The Curies. What made it radioactive? The disintegration of the atom. There was a good deal of vocabulary testing. For example, "The adjective *livid* means: (1) red; (2) furious; (3) illuminated; (4) pale?" Neal checked 4, and knew that he was right.

General knowledge was followed by general math. Neal approached this exam with the same feeling of apprehension. Again he feared to face the unknown, the unfriendly. Unknown? He knew logarithms and quadratic equations—he had made friends with them early in the morning between 6 and 7 A.M.

The gadgets used to test co-ordination in the physical-aptitude exam were new to him, but the basic facts behind them were familiar. The sharp eye fixed the object, the conditioned nerve reacted, and the result was equivalent to a well-timed lateral on the football field or a reflex volley in tennis. Neal left March Field with a lighter step, and was carefully confident as he faced the College Boards.

Then came the wait for the results of all these tests. In this time of tension some of Neal's confidence ebbed. But training for the Air Force physical continued to keep him busy and to lessen his worry. Finally the notice came.

Opening the envelope with fumbling fingers, Neal stared at the marks, eyes wide with anxiety. Summed up, the scores said one wonderful word, "Qualified!"

He let out a whoop, then sobered up, remembering that he was only the third alternate. Ahead of him in priority stood three other candidates—the second alternate, the first alternate, and the principal. Undoubtedly they, too, had qualified.

Undoubtedly? Without warning another letter arrived from the office of Congressman Burton. "Dear Neal Davis, Congratulations on qualifying for the Air Force Academy. I am sure you will be pleased to know that you are now the second alternate."

Second alternate! That could only mean that one of the nominees with a top priority had failed somewhere along the line. Neal was now in third place. It was like a pennant race, with all three teams racing toward the final test—the rigorous Air Force physical exam in May.

On his second trip to March Field, Neal's mental

attitude changed. He knew now what the fourth and final period of the Thanksgiving Day game had hinted at; he knew that he had what it takes. He had proved it not only to himself but to exacting examiners. There was just one thing wrong with this great effort; it had come too late. If it had been made a year earlier he might well have been the first alternate or even the principal.

On his first trip to March Field Neal had been so anxious to pass the general-aptitude exam that he had paid little attention to his rivals. Now, as the candidates were called alphabetically for their physicals, Neal, under D, was the first of the top three to go through—the other two being Dell Hubbard, the principal, and John Sandys, the first alternate. Neal, watching and waiting, had an opportunity to size up his opponents. Dell Hubbard of Bakersfield was a tall, good-looking self-confident type, who reminded Neal of Don Latimer. John Sandys of Riverside was more like Oliver Jensen, but he also looked sufficiently fit.

As he waited for the results of the exam, Neal felt like a sub on the bench, hoping to get into a game dominated by two veterans. He knew that unless one of them flunked, his services would not be needed.

Out came Dell Hubbard, the principal, as self-assured as ever. It was obvious that he had passed the physical with flying colors. Other nominees joined them. They, too, had passed, but Neal wasn't worried about them, for they were beneath him in priority. The candidate he worried about was John Sandys. What had happened to him?

Someone brought them the news. John Sandys had failed the exacting eye exam and, knowing that he was disqualified, had gone home. Neal felt a flash of pity, followed by a surge of elation. He was now the first alternate!

He was still elated as he left March Field, but it did not last long. The next period of waiting gradually sapped his high spirits. After all, he was not the principal. It was true that the Falcon had got in as a qualified alternate, but that was a condition that called for vacancies in the entering class. How was Neal to know whether or not such a condition now existed? He could not know until the last minute.

Neal felt that he was warming the bench again, waiting on pins and needles. He had the discouraging feeling that he would always be an alternate and never a principal. It was all the more discouraging, because he knew that he was better prepared now than ever.

The tension mounted with each mail delivery. He would seize the mail and sort it with moist fingers. There would be a letter for his mother from his older brother Joe, now serving his time in the Navy, or a letter from a summer-tourist friend to his kid sister Karen. But there was no long envelope, marked "Official Business," from the Air Force Academy or Congressman Burton. Neal's hopes began to fade. If he missed the mail he would call up from high school at the lunch hour and ask anxiously, "Any mail for me, Mom?"

"No, Neal. Sorry." His mother was sympathetic. "Don't worry, son. It will come."

How could he help worrying? he asked himself. Everything—his whole life—seemed to depend now on an official *yes* or *no* from Washington, D. C. or Colorado Springs. The suspense was terrible. It wasn't fair, Neal complained one night at dinner to his father, a quiet gray-haired man with glasses.

His father smiled sympathetically. "You'd be surprised, Neal, if you knew how many lives seem to depend on a *yes* or *no* from Washington. This just happens to be the first time you've experienced it."

Neal nodded. Now that he thought of it, this was probably true. A *yes* or *no* from Washington had put part of the big aviation company into the missile business, and had moved the Davis family from northern to southern California. Decisions made in Washington and Moscow were affecting the lives of people from Armenia to Zululand. He, Neal, wasn't the only one affected, and he might derive some comfort from that fact, considering it on a high, detached level.

But it was hard to keep it up there, high and detached. It had a way of coming down to a low, personal, emotional level that continually disturbed his sleep and tightened the muscles of his stomach when mail time came.

"Any mail for me, Mom?"

"No, son. Sorry."

That was on a Friday. He went to a movie in the evening and tried to forget his tensions as he watched a foreign agent—male—in a trench coat, pursue a foreign agent—female—in a fur coat.

In the morning, after a sleep broken by waking periods of worry, he was starting his homework and wondering if the work was worthwhile, when the phone rang. "This is Western Union. We have a telegram for Neal Davis from Washington, D. C."

"I'm Neal Davis," he said, and his voice squeaked.

Western Union ignored the squeak. It went on, cold and matter-of-fact. "I'll read it to you. 'Congratulations. You have been accepted by the Air Force Academy as a qualified alternate.' Signed, 'Congressman James Burton.'"

Neal couldn't believe it. He made the Western Union operator repeat the message. The Western Union operator was a girl, he finally realized, as she repeated the message for the third time. Asked for a fourth rendition, she refused. "Look," she said. "I'll mail you a copy."

"Don't bother," cried Neal. "I'll come right down to the office and pick it up myself."

He carried it around in his pocket, fishing it out from

time to time to confirm his happiness. It was true. What a lucky break!

Break? Yes, but it was like one of those lucky breaks in football, the kind you set up by extra effort and practiced skill. It didn't just happen; it was made. It was true, the old saw, the old chestnut—life was like a game. But what had Coach Grigsby added? "They keep moving back the goal posts."

Now just what did that signify? Did it mean that every time you scored a touchdown, a new game began? Couldn't you just stand here in the end zone, listening happily to the cheers, accepting the congratulations? No, you couldn't. The goal posts were being moved back. The new game was about to begin.

The new game began on July 1 in Colorado, at an altitude several thousand feet above sea level and several hundred miles northeast of Neal's home town in southern California. Carrying his suitcase, he changed buses in Colorado Springs. About ten miles to the north the bus entered a campus of 10,000 acres. Here, high on mesa land, rose the brilliantly modern glass-and-steel buildings of the Air Force Academy, gleaming against the green background of mountains, the pine-studded slopes of the Rampart Range of the Rockies.

Suitcase in hand, Neal found himself standing with a dazzled group of recruits in an immense quadrangle. The building that formed the north end of the quadrangle was six glass stories high and looked longer than four football fields.

"That's Vandenberg Hall," someone said. "It's a dormitory."

"A dormitory?" twanged a nasal voice. "It's an over-grown goldfish bowl, and we're going to be the gold-fish."

Who made that irreverent remark? Neal turned, and found himself staring at the most striking face he had seen in some time.

A very close haircut, almost bald at the temples, re-vealed two ears that seemed large enough to be owned by an elephant. Unbalanced by this super crew cut, the youth's face seemed to stick far out in front, like the figures on the bowsprits of old sailing ships. It was, in a way, as if the features had run a race to escape the ears. The spadelike nose had won, the thin lips had come in second, the bony chin third. Though defeated, the chin had not given up. It was still jutting out determinedly, and might someday win. The thin mouth had the same sort of doggedness that character-ized the chin, and above the spadelike nose dark-brown eyes flickered, like a kaleidoscope of glass panels revolv-ing in front of a spotlight, quickly reflecting the change in moods.

Neal was wearing a sport shirt under a jacket, but he wondered if he should have worn a regular shirt with a tie. Elephant Ears was wearing simply a sport shirt; no jacket covered his bony shoulders. His shirt had no sleeves, but it did have tails, which flapped outside the trousers when their owner walked. Neal, watching, wondered if the ears would flap, too, and was a little surprised when they didn't.

In ordinary circumstances Neal might have edged away from this apparition, but in his present state of awe and apprehension he was glad for any company. Now the nasal voice twanged an introduction. "My name's Hoyt—Ethan Hoyt. I'm from Portland."

Mechanically Neal put out his hand. "I'm Neal Davis from Fairview—southern California."

"Never heard of it," said Ethan Hoyt. The brown eyes flickered, and the thin lips twitched, either in humor or sarcasm—or both.

Slightly unbalanced by the bluntness of this remark, Neal lurched into another inadvertent admission. "As a matter of fact, I'm really from northern California— San Francisco."

"That's better," said Hoyt. Again the brown eyes flickered, and the thin mouth twitched.

Better? thought Neal indignantly. Well, yes, he had always thought so. But by what right did this clown from Portland set himself up as an arbiter of regional distinctions? Still off balance, Neal blurted out, "What's so hot about Portland, Oregon?"

"I wouldn't know," said Ethan Hoyt dryly. "I'm from 'way down East—Portland, Maine."

Maine! An almost forgotten state from Neal's geographical point of view. 'Way down East. East of what? The answer would probably be some dry, thin-lipped, sarcastic Yankee witticism. Neal passed up the question. In any case, Maine was 'way down East to a Californian, who thought of any city on the other side of the Mississippi as "east."

Neal took another look at Ethan Hoyt—a guarded look. His shirttails were flapping, his eyes were blinking, his elephant ears were standing out rather like radar antennae listening for enemy signals. "Here they come," he said.

"Who?" said Neal.

"Our enemies, the upperclassmen," said the Yankee.

Neal heard it now, the rhythmic cadence of marching feet. A small group of cadets, as straight as ramrods and immaculately uniformed, were marching across the quadrangle in the direction of the recruits.

"Just take it easy, Davis," warned the Yankee, "and do what you're told. Don't forget—you're just a doolie."

Neal felt more confused than ever. He resented being called by his last name—in California everyone got on a first-name basis immediately—and he had no idea what a *doolie* was. He didn't want to ask, but he had to find out.

"We're both doolies," explained the Yankee, "freshmen, fourth classmen. These characters coming are third classmen—sophomores."

"Oh," said Neal. He wanted almost desperately to say something intelligent, if not brilliant, but he was still dazzled by the setting and confused by the 'way-down-East style of Ethan Hoyt.

He looked around at the other doolies. Perhaps there was someone else, a more normal recruit, who could help straighten out this situation. There. That face looked familiar. Who was he? Why, it was the good-looking principal who had been so self-assured during the exams at March Field. What was his name now? Oh yes, Dell Hubbard.

But that had been Dell Hubbard at March Field, California. Dell Hubbard here at the Academy looked just as awed and apprehensive as any other doolie. He would be no help. Moreover, the upperclassmen were now within range. They were breaking ranks, singling out victims, and the cadet standing in front of Neal had a face as unyielding as a slab of cement. Suddenly it cracked with a command.

"At-ten-SHUN!"

Neal had expected it, but the explosion of the order numbed him.

"You, mister!" barked Cement Face.

Me! thought Neal. Get to attention, quick!

"Put those shoulders back!"

They *were* back. Did they think he was double-jointed?

"Suck in that stomach!"

What stomach? Diet and exercise had practically eliminated it. It couldn't possibly be protruding.

"Pull in that chin!"

It is in. It's just about touching the collar of my sport shirt.

"You're a cadet now, mister," said Cement Face.

"Yes, sir." I didn't think I was a jumping jack.

"From now on, mister, you don't *turn* corners, you *square* them."

Square corners?

"Like this, mister." Cement Face stepped off a few paces smartly, then clicked his heels, made a right turn at what looked like a precise forty-five-degree angle, and stepped out smartly again. So that, thought Neal, is a square corner. It's going to take a lot of the fun out of strolling.

Cement Face was zeroing in again like a dive bomber. "You don't *walk* across this area, mister—you double time across it, like this." The upperclassman broke into a brisk jog. "All right, mister, on the double. Hup-two-three-four!"

Neal jogged.

"Halt! At ease! Not like that, mister." Neal had stopped and gone into a grateful slump. "Like this!"

Cement Face snapped to attention, then smoothly slipped into a spread stance, feet apart, arms locked behind his back. His shoulders were still very straight and his chin and stomach well in.

There isn't much ease in "at ease," thought Neal. But the brief break did give him time to glance sideways—he was learning how to glance sideways, moving only his eyeballs—to see how the other doolies were making out. Dell Hubbard seemed to have shrunk into a shell. Ethan Hoyt was sweating it out under the guidance of another upperclassman with a southern accent.

"Pull up your landing gear, mistuh!"

"What, sir?" twanged Ethan Hoyt.

"Tuck in those shirt tay-uls!"

"Yes, sir!"

The Yankee's bony hands reached for his shirttails and hastily stuffed them inside his trousers. Then he went back to attention with a snap that surprised Neal. It looked as if the Yankee had been practicing. He was standing surprisingly straight, a posture that made him just as tall as Neal. His bony shoulders were braced, his bony chin was in, and the expression on his face was completely solemn. Gone were all traces of sarcasm and irreverence. The Yankee was obviously playing it cool.

"Where are you from, mistuh?"

"Portland, Maine, sir."

"Portland, Maine, mistuh?" the southerner repeated with mock incredulity. Now he put his hands on his hips, spread his feet, and grinned. "That makes you just about one-hundred-per-cent Yankee, doesn't it, mistuh?"

"Yes, sir," said Ethan Hoyt.

The southerner continued to grin. "All right, mis-tuh, ah'll forgive yuh. But just tell me this—who won the War Between the States?"

Ethan Hoyt hesitated, and Neal thought, This south-erner is real corn—ripe and golden. Corn Pone would be a good name for him.

The Yankee was answering with a straight face. "The South, sir," he said.

Cement Face, the upperclassman standing near Neal, laughed. Corn Pone frowned. Apparently he had planned on using the right answer as a springboard for several Confederate remarks. By giving the wrong answer, the Yankee had crossed up the Confederate. Somewhat frustrated, Corn Pone began to circle his victim like a detective inspecting a suspect in the police line-up. Now Corn Pone caught sight of the protuber-ant ears and frowned again. Everything had been pulled in but those ears. Corn Pone glared at the offending appurtenances. He seemed to be stymied. He could bark, "Pull in those ears!" but it was highly doubtful if the Yankee could carry out such a com-mand. Corn Pone, still frowning and frustrated, moved on in his encirclement. The Yankee's ears seemed to move—they *were* moving. The Yankee was wiggling them!

Neal was amazed and apprehensive. If Corn Pone saw what was happening, the Yankee would get his ears pinned back. But it was Cement Face who spotted the insubordinate ears. He grinned.

Neal was encouraged. Cement Face was human, and perhaps even friendly. Neal smiled too. It was a mistake.

"Wipe that smile off your face, mister!"

Friendly? Cement Face was about as friendly as a mountain lion from the Rampart Range.

Corn Pone looked up, caught on, and snapped, "Stop wiggling those ears!"

That did it. Cement Face let out another laugh before he could stop it, and he even allowed Neal a quick grin. Other upperclassmen in the vicinity relaxed their stern vigilance, if only for a moment. The Yankee had scored; he had lured his tormentor into a ridiculous command.

And how was the hero of this incident taking his triumph? Straight and solemn. His ears were still, his eyes did not flicker, the movement of the muscles around his mouth gave nothing away. Corn Pone could circle the Yankee menacingly, slandering his stomach, shoulders, and chin. But those ears, though no longer wiggling, stood out defiantly, a Union flag flying in Corn Pone's Confederate face. He chose not to mention them again; once was enough.

"Attention in the area! Attention in the area!"

The doolies were listening to a command from

another source, the stern but more impersonal voice of the public-address system.

"All fourth classmen are to report at once to the Administration Building for room assignment.

"I say again, all fourth classmen are to report at once to the Administration Building for room assignment.

"Security Flight out."

Gadzooks! said Neal to himself. We're surrounded! The voices of the enemy are everywhere—Cement Face, Corn Pone, and now Security Flight on the PA system.

"Fo-whad harch!" snapped Cement Face. "Hup-two-three-four!"

CHAPTER 8

Neal was listening anxiously as names were called alphabetically. Adamowski. Bernstein. Brinkley. Connelly. *Davis*. Somehow your own name always sounded louder than the others. Gentry. *Hoyt. Hubbard*. Those names also jarred the eardrums.

Doolies were being paired off according to height and geographical opposites—Michigan with Louisiana, California with Maine, Hoyt with Davis. Gadzooks! If anyone had asked Neal not so long ago whom he would have chosen for a roommate, one of the last persons on his list would have been someone like the sardonic Yankee from Portland, Maine. But after the events that had just taken place, Ethan Hoyt seemed like an old friend—an eccentric, to be sure—but an ally just the same.

When they had carried their suitcases up to the room they would share, Neal admired the newness and neatness of the furnishings—the beds, the desks, the chairs

—two of each—and the picture window with an impos-
ing view of the Rocky Mountains. Each room also had
its own adjoining lavatory. But what was the eccentric
Yankee examining? The electrical outlets!

From an unimpressive fiberboard suitcase the Yankee had brought forth a small, neat tool kit. Out of it
had come an amazing screw driver. When unscrewed,
the handle of this tool spawned several more screw-
drivers of various sizes. Selecting one, Ethan Hoyt,
with amazingly agile fingers, went to work on a wall
switch.

"What in the name of Colorado are you doing?"
asked Neal.

"What does it look like I'm doing?" said the Yankee.
"I'm checking the wiring. First thing I always do in
a new place."

"Why?" asked Neal.

"Tell you later," said the Yankee. "I've got to hurry.
The secret police may be here any minute."

Bats in his belfry, said Neal to himself. He's as nutty
as a fruitcake. Aloud he said, "Of course it's a good
idea to check the wiring. Everyone knows that half the
homes in America are badly wired."

"This is no home," said the Yankee. "It's an institu-
tion." Then he gave a grunt. "A-ha!" he said. "I'm
glad to see they didn't install the old flush-type tumbler
switch, but used the tap-action type instead."

"So am I," said Neal, going along with the gag. "I never did like the old flush-tap tumbler type."

"You mean old flush-type tumbler, don't you?" said the Yankee, with a suspicious glance.

"Of course," said Neal. "A slip of the tongue. Of course I meant the old flish-tom trumbler tripe."

"Humph." The Yankee belittled the witticism and replaced the plate on the wall switch. Then he moved to the doorway, spotted something outside, and beckoned. "Look," he said. "A control board. Boy! This place has more wiring than Westinghouse. Know what each of those lights stands for?"

"Nope," said Neal.

"Neither do I," said Ethan flatly. The Yankee was squinting up at the glass panel on the corridor wall. "I heard," he said, "that each light on the board stands for the uniform of the day. But that may just be hearsay. You don't believe hearsay, do you, Davis?"

"Of course not," said Neal, still somewhat nettled by the use of the last name. Back home they would have been on a first-name basis long ago. This down-Easter was a cold fish.

The Yankee was now pointing with his screw driver to a small square grill over a vent. "Ten to one that's the squawk box," he said.

"What's that?" said Neal.

"The PA system," said the Yankee airily. "Remember? We heard it outside." He now gave an imitation in a sonorous voice. " 'Attention in the area! Attention in the area! When you hear the signal, blow your noses. I say again, when you hear the signal, blow your noses. Security Flight out.' "

In explaining something the Yankee managed to make it more confusing. So many new and strange things were happening that Neal would only be slightly surprised if Security Flight did tell him when to blow his nose.

"Security Flight is just like Superman," the Yankee was saying. "He is everywhere all at once. The wonders of electricity are cleverly used here." He led the way back into the room and, murmuring and mumbling, was now exploring the wiring in the lavatory. "Mm-hmn, another tap-action wall switch. Uh-hmn, an outlet for electric razors. Hmn, a very convenient air vent. Yes, Davis, it will do."

"What will do?" said Neal.

"The way things are arranged," said the Yankee. Again using his screw driver as a pointer, he said, "See this outlet? Plug in here, get your juice, and run the wire behind the clothes hamper, concealing it from the victim's view. Unscrew that grill over the air vent, insert the vital object, replace the grill, and, as we used to say at Portland Prep, Q.E.D."

"Why do you insist on talking in riddles?" said Neal impatiently. "Why are you so interested in all this electrical stuff? What are you planning to do—short-circuit the plant?"

Ethan Hoyt crooked his finger around his nose. "Later, Davis. The explanations come later. Now is the time to look over the lay of the land."

But Neal persisted. He was tired of swinging wildly at change-of-pace pitches. "Do you plan to tap in on the PA system and pretend you're Security Flight?"

"Sh-h! No!" said the Yankee with a sharp whisper. "But not so loud, Davis."

Neal lowered his voice. "O.K., but why all the mystery, Hoyt?" He had decided to return the compliment and call the Yankee by *his* last name.

"For good and sundry reasons," said the Yankee. "In the first place, Davis, we've just met. I don't know what you're like. I must go slowly—New England reserve, you know."

"I don't know what you're like either," said Neal indignantly, "except that you're—well, sort of a—uh—"

"A screwball?" said the Yankee. "No, Davis, let me tell you what I am." He smiled in his usual thin and sardonic way. "I'm a rebel, Davis. I was a rebel at Portland Prep, and I'm going to be a rebel here at the Air Force Academy."

"You picked a fine place," said Neal sarcastically.

"You misunderstand me," said the Yankee. "I don't mean that I'm going to rebel violently and stupidly. I intend to rebel cleverly and with subtlety. In other words, when the upperclassmen tell me to pull back my shoulders, I'll do it, but at the same time I may wiggle my ears. Understand?"

"Sort of," said Neal. He had to admit that the ear wiggling had worked. It had made Cement Face laugh; that was something.

"Look at my haircut," said the Yankee. "It shouldn't happen to a sheep, should it?"

Neal grinned. "No," he said, "it shouldn't. But it happened to you."

"Right," said the Yankee, "and it's going to happen to you, too."

"Will it be that bad?" said Neal.

"That bad," said the Yankee. "But it can't happen to me, because it's already happened. They can't inflict it on me, Davis. I've already inflicted it on myself. See? It deprives them of the satisfaction of destroying —ahem—my good looks." The Yankee smiled wanly. "I have already destroyed them. Understand?"

"Sort of," said Neal.

"You noticed, perhaps, that my shirttails were outside my trousers. I did that on purpose, Davis. It gave the uppperclassman something to correct, something obvious that even a nitwit wouldn't miss. It pleased him to pounce on those offensive shirttails."

Neal frowned. "But I didn't know you were trying to please upperclassmen, Hoyt."

"I'm not," said the mad Yankee. "I'm just trying

to keep them off balance. If they become too frustrated, Davis, they become dangerous. We're at war, and every skirmish counts toward the final victory."

"At war with whom?" said Neal almost irritably. He was tiring. He had swung and missed too often.

"With the third classmen," said the Yankee, "those gentlemen who were giving us the works out there in the area."

"You mean Cement Face and Corn Pone?" said Neal.

"Who?" It was the Yankee's turn to be puzzled.

Neal smiled. He had scored, if only in a small way. "Just nicknames," he said. "The guy who braced me had a face like a slab of cement. The guy who braced you had a deep southern accent that reminded me of corn pone."

"Ah," said the Yankee. "Ah, yes. Cement Face and Corn Pone. Very good, Davis. You're catching on."

"To what?" said Neal.

"To the subtle rebellion, Davis. Take a slightly derogatory nickname, such as Cement Face or Corn Pone. You pin it on an enemy, it spreads, and it gives you a certain satisfaction every time you hear it. That's the right spirit, Davis. Keep it up. It won't be long before you'll be ready to enlist."

"In what?" said Neal.

"In the Underground, Davis—the Resistance Movement. A war is going to be fought here. In fact, the first shots have already been fired. But you don't believe me, do you?" The Yankee's eye flickered, and his ears wiggled.

Neal smiled. "I'm not convinced yet," he said.

"Why not, Davis?" The Yankee frowned. "Let me ask you a question. Did you come here from high school or prep school?"

"High school," said Neal.

"That explains it," said the Yankee triumphantly. "I fought this type of war before at Portland Prep. I know what we're up against. It's ruthless, Davis, and relentless."

"Rattlesnakes!" said Neal derisively.

"And coyotes too," said the Yankee. He put his screw driver back into his tool kit. Then with loving hands he rearranged its contents—the versatile screw driver, the pliers, a small hammer, and a saw. "Maybe you misunderstand me," said the Yankee. "Possibly you're thinking of physical hazing—the old-fashioned kind of school warfare. That's out of date. This is the new kind—much more deadly, much harder to take. They're going to try to brainwash us, Davis, and we must fight back."

"Nonsense," said Neal. It might not be nonsense, but he didn't like the idea of the Yankee's being so omniscient.

Ethan Hoyt shrugged his shoulders. "Have it your own way, Davis, while you still can. It won't last, I assure you." The Yankee closed his tool kit. "I wonder

where I could hide this," he said, as if to himself.
"They'll be searching every corner of the room."

He's as crazy as a loon, thought Neal. All that jazz
about war and the Underground. Ridiculous.

"Things are already shaping up in my mind," said
the Yankee. "We must plan now while we still have
time, before the struggle becomes intense. Project one,
priority A. A false bottom in the clothes hamper—that
would fool them."

Fool whom? said Neal silently, the attendants from
the insane asylum? It was doubtful if the Yankee
would fool them. What was he saying now?

"Which bed do you want, Davis, which desk, which
chair? There are two of everything here."

But only *one* lunatic, thought Neal. And yet now,
as they divided up the furniture, the Yankee seemed
rational and reasonable.

"Attention in the area! Attention in the area!" The
squawk box had come alive. Neal listened nervously.

"All fourth classmen report to the Administration
Building immediately. I say again, all fourth classmen
report to the Administration Building immediately.
Security Flight out."

The Yankee smiled. "The second skirmish of the
war, Davis. We are about to be processed. Isn't that a
nice word for it? *Processed!* How would you like to
have your hair cut, Davis? Long on the sides, perhaps,
with just a little off the top? What kind of clothes do

you want to wear? How about a nice tweed jacket and a pair of gray flannels?"

Neal said nothing. They were both hurrying out of the room into the long corridor. Down they hustled, down the corridor, down and around a handsome spiral staircase, and out into the area.

"Don't forget, Davis, we have to trot here; on the double! Hup-two-three-four! They've got us on the run already."

Have they? Neal asked himself. Maybe the Yankee was right; maybe there was some sense in his nonsense, some shrewd New England streak in what seemed like insanity. Certainly Ethan Hoyt could conform when he had to. As they lined up for their uniforms, he was as humble and obedient as any other doolie. Silently, submissively, he accepted the khaki shirts and trousers.

Neal was disappointed. Where were the glamorous sky-blue uniforms that the Falcon Paul Gregson had sported? These duds looked like work clothes, and Neal whispered as much to Ethan Hoyt.

"What did you expect?" the Yankee whispered back. "Dress whites?"

The name the uniforms **had** brought up—Paul Gregson—produced another question. Where was the Falcon? Neal decided to consult the New England oracle, Ethan Hoyt. As always, the oracle was ready with an answer. Was Paul Gregson a junior, a second classman? Then he would be on leave—perhaps in Europe.

Second classmen could trade their summer leave for a tour of Allied Air Force bases in countries like England and Italy.

And how did the Yankee know so much? Ethan Hoyt smiled smugly. He had simply boned up on the Academy before coming to it, had read all about its rules and regulations. He had been determined not to arrive at the Academy as fearful and bewildered as he had once arrived at Portland Prep.

Am I fearful and bewildered? Neal asked himself. He certainly was bewildered—and apprehensive—as he went through the next step in processing, the Academy haircut.

To the barber the back of Neal's head was a runway, the electric clippers a jet. Vrooommm. The clippers took off, spraying hair this way and that. Circling the head, the clippers landed on the left temple. Vrooommm. They took off again, spraying another shower of hair over the white towel. After a third take-off from the right temple, the barber smiled and said, "There you are, mister."

Neal looked in the mirror and quailed. It was a shocking sight, but he managed a rueful grin.

"Next!"

The Yankee slipped into the chair, ears wiggling, eyes flickering. The barber stared.

"Wait a minute, mister," he said. "You've been here already."

"No, sir," said the Yankee.

"You sure you didn't get that haircut here, mister?"

"Positive, sir," said the Yankee, with a twitch of his thin lips.

"But it's a standard Air Force Academy haircut, mister."

"Is that so?" said the Yankee. "Then it must be a coincidence. Back where I come from this is known as a typical down-East haircut."

"Next!" said the barber. The Yankee had won another skirmish in the war.

Outside the barbershop he joined Neal and said, "Now you look just as funny as I do."

"Thanks," said Neal dryly.

"Processing," twanged the Yankee. "Uniformity, conformity. Everyone must look alike, act alike. We are being poured into molds, Davis. The upperclassmen will cook us in their crucible, and we shall emerge as little tin soldiers. How does that future sound to you, Davis?"

"Unpleasant," said Neal.

A voice from the rear interrupted. "Davis! Neal Davis!"

Cement Face! Neal gave a start and snapped to attention.

"At ease," said the voice. "It's only me, Dell Hubbard."

"Oh," said Neal. He turned and stared. Gone with

the hair were the good looks. Revealed by the barber's ruthless shears was a knobby head with buttonlike ears. "Sorry," said Neal. "I didn't recognize you for a moment."

Dell Hubbard smiled weakly. "Same to you," he said. Then, lowering his voice, he added, "Brother! These haircuts are strictly from Alcatraz."

"An interesting observation," said the Yankee. "Introduce me to your friend, Davis."

"Oh, sure," said Neal. "Dell Hubbard, Ethan Hoyt."

"Glad to know you, Hubbard," said Hoyt.

"Same to you," said Hubbard. He seemed nervous and hurried. "Well—uh—nice to have seen you both. I'd better get back to my room. There may be an inspection or something. So long."

He hurried off. When he reached the quadrangle, he broke into a trot, and double timed across the vast enclosure.

"An interesting victim of upperclassman warfare," said the Yankee.

"He was the principal at my entrance exams," explained Neal. "I was just the second alternate, but I got a lucky break." Lucky? he added to himself. Then he said aloud, "Say, Hoyt, we've reached the area. We'd better jog."

"Of course," said the Yankee. "We submit physically, but we rebel mentally."

They broke into a trot. "Dell Huh-Hubbard," said the Yankee, the trot affecting his air supply and splitting his words into huh-huh syllables. "The huh-high-school hero type. The big shot at podunk huh-high. Suddenly he's zero at the Acad-huh-my. Quite huh-shock."

"Hup," said Neal.

"He resents hut," puffed the Yankee.

"Hup," said Neal.

"More than most," said the Yankee. "He huh-had farther to fall."

"Hup," said Neal.

They jogged silently for a stretch, and then the Yankee said, "Might-huh make use of Hub-bard."

"Huh-how?" said Neal.

The Yankee didn't answer. His breath had apparently become too short. All that came out of him now was a huh-huh without words. Was the Yankee's brain working out some plot against the upperclassmen, or was he just out of breath?

Neal couldn't tell—and didn't care much. Life as a doolie was confusing enough without further complications concerning the comedowns of high-school big shots.

▏▏▏▏▏▏▏▏▏▏▏▏▏▏▏▏▏▏ *CHAPTER 9* ▏▏▏▏▏▏▏▏▏▏▏▏▏▏▏▏▏▏▏▏

The life of a doolie was breathlessly confusing, disconcerting, discouraging. Neal hadn't come to the Academy to fight a war against upperclassmen—or what was worse, to be drafted for that war by Ethan Hoyt, the mad Yankee from Portland, Maine. As he jogged and stumbled through the bewildering afternoon, Neal took hurried glances into the future, searching for something pleasant.

Football? That was far, far away in the fall. It was only summer now. As for tennis, there was no time for it.

But wait. What was this event, the next on the busy schedule? Food, dinner in the dining hall, the joy of eating! Surely during dinner an armistice would be declared, and the tyrants and slaves could break bread together peacefully. Food had a way of making friends out of enemies. Matters that were sore subjects on empty stomachs became laughable, as the healthily hungry were fed.

Look at this dining hall. Magnificent! As beautiful as an enormous and translucent birthday cake. Admire those marvelous glass walls, and through them that splendid view of the Colorado landscape, mountainous slopes studded with evergreens.

"How about it, Hoyt?" whispered Neal to his comrade-in-arms, as they marched in. "I'll bet dear old Portland Prep had nothing like this."

"No," admitted the Yankee, apparently awed. "It didn't."

"And waiters too," said Neal. "We're going to be waited on. How about that?"

"Hmm," said the Yankee, a suspicious "hmm." He was walking warily, like a soldier crossing a mine field, his antenna ears wiggling, as if trying to tune in on an enemy wave length.

"What's the matter?" kidded Neal. "Worried about the wiring?"

"It isn't the wiring that worries me," said the Yankee. "Ah!" he exclaimed. Then, lowering his voice, "There they are."

"Who?"

"Our enemies," said the Yankee darkly. "Cement Face and Corn Pone."

Enemies? thought Neal. Impossible. A dining hall of such size and magnificence could not nourish enemies—it had to promote friendships. Surely even Cement Face and Corn Pone would mellow in this congenial atmosphere. See how hospitable they looked at their table, Cement Face at one end, Corn Pone at the other.

"And we're in between," said the Yankee glumly. "We're going to be whipsawed."

"Nonsense," whispered Neal. "Why, look, they're even smiling. Isn't it wonderful what food will do for a sour puss?"

"Yeah," said the Yankee skeptically.

"Good evening, Mr. Davis." It was Cement Face speaking, smiling. "Please be seated."

"Thank you, sir," said Neal, and with a glance at the Yankee that said "I told you so," Neal sat down comfortably, hungrily. The armistice is on, he sighed with relief. Three square meals could be eaten every day in civilized peace.

But what was Cement Face saying softly but firmly? "No, Mr. Davis, don't sit quite so comfortably. Sit up straight on the front edge of your chair, Mr. Davis. That's it, *straight,* with those shoulders back and that chin in! That's better."

Neal groaned. The armistice was over.

Corn Pone turned to the Yankee. "Mistuh Hoyt," he said, "ah hereby appoint you Cold Pilot in charge of all cold beverages—milk, iced tea, iced coffee, and ice watah. Got it, mistuh?"

"Yes, sir," said the Yankee, sitting up straight on the edge of his chair.

Corn Pone continued. "Ah want no one at either end of the ramp to go thirsty for a cold beverage. Understand, mistuh?"

"Yes, sir," said the Yankee.

"All right, Cold Pilot, you may start servin' the iced beverages. Mr. Blackstone!" Corn Pone spoke to his opposite number. "Mr. Blackstone, can mah Cold Pilot fly you up a coolin' beverage of some kind?"

Blackstone, alias Cement Face, smiled pleasantly. "Iced tea would be fine, Mr. Willoughby."

"One iced tea!" barked Corn Pone to the Yankee. "Fly 'er up!"

"Yes, sir!" said the Yankee. Hurriedly he poured the iced tea and passed it.

"Mr. Willoughby." Cement Face was speaking. "Could my Hot Pilot fly you down a warm beverage of some kind?"

"Ah do believe a cup of hot coffee would hit the spot, Mr. Blackstone."

"Of course," said Cement Face. Abruptly changing his pleasant tone and face, he barked, "Hot Pilot!"

"You mean me, sir?" said Neal nervously.

"I mean you," snapped Cement Face. "One cup of coffee down the ramp!"

"Yes, sir," said Neal. As he poured and passed the coffee, he thought, The Yankee was right. It *is* war.

There is no such thing as an armistice. We're in for it.

"Cold Pilot! One iced tea!"

"Yes, sir," said Ethan Hoyt.

"Hot Pilot! One cocoa!"

"Yes, sir," said Neal.

"Cold Pilot! One milk!"

"Yes, sir," said the Yankee.

"Hot Pilot! One more coffee!"

"Yes, sir."

Sitting up straight on the edge of his chair, Neal poured and passed, poured and passed, and tried, between orders, to eat some of his cold consommé. Gosh, it was good! But it was gone. The waiter had taken it.

"Hot Pilot! One coffee!"

"Yes, sir." Pour and pass. Ummm. Roast lamb. Delicious. And mashed potatoes with gravy. And string beans. Yumm.

"Hot Pilot! One cocoa!"

"Yes, sir." Pour and pass.

"Hot Pilot! Flame out that empty pot of coffee 'cross country to the hangar."

"Flame it out, sir?" asked Neal.

"Send it out with the waiter, mister."

"To the hangar, sir?" said Neal, still confused.

"The kitchen, mister."

"Yes, sir." Hey! Where did the meat and potatoes

go? Gadzooks! This restaurant was like an assembly line, with food on the conveyor belt. If you took your eye off it for a minute it was gone.

At that moment Neal vowed that if ever he met that clown, Cement Face, on the football field, he would hit him so hard he would never again think of hazing a doolie. It was an inspiring thought for the future. Unfortunately, the future, varsity football, was a long way off. Neal grew glum, but then another thought revived him—freshman football in the fall. That would save him. Ah, the thrill of a broken-field run! He would show them. He would fulfill the promise made in the final few minutes of the Greenfield game. He was bigger now and stronger. He should make an outstanding back on the freshman team. That would make up for all the indignities he was having to suffer now as a doolie.

The prospect of playing freshman football in a few months carried Neal through to the dessert—rice pudding with raisins. Umm.

"Cold Pilot! One iced tea! And stop wigglin' those eahs!"

Corn Pone had caught on to Ethan Hoyt's strategy, which had worked so well in the quadrangle.

"It's an uncontrollable nerve reflex, sir," said the Yankee, his eyes flickering.

"You'll have to learn to control it, mistuh," snapped Corn Pone. "Uncontrollable nerve reflexes aren't al-

lowed at the Academy, are they, Mr. Blackstone?"
Corn Pone changed his voice to a pleasant conversational tone.

"No indeed, Mr. Willoughby," said Cement Face.
"Hot Pilot! Another cup of coffee for Mr. Willoughby."

"Yes, sir." It's my turn to try sabotage, thought Neal, to help my comrade-in-arms. The Yankee tried the ear wiggling trick and failed, so I'll purposely spill the coffee.

It wasn't hard to do and make it seem accidental. He simply let his left hand shake as he poured and passed. The cup jiggled, the coffee spilled.

"Oops," said Neal. "Sorry, sir." That, he thought, will teach these wise guys to make me Hot Pilot and put me under so much pressure.

But what was Cement Face saying, in a mockingly solicitous tone? "That's all right, Mr. Davis. Just wipe it up, every drop, and then pour another cup." He was smiling. "I appreciate your problems, Mr. Davis. It's very difficult to pour hot coffee and cocoa constantly and to eat at the same time. I was a Hot Pilot once myself." Cement Face ate some rice pudding and sighed, "Delicious!" He wiped his lips and went on. "I used to spill the hot drinks too, Mr. Davis, but I soon found out that cleaning up after spilling took more time than pouring and passing properly. Waiter!" Cement Face intervened. "I don't think Mr.

Davis has quite finished his rice pudding. Would you give him another minute, please?"

"Thank you, sir," said Neal, swallowing his pride with some of his pudding.

"Not at all," said Cement Face with a sardonic smile. "An upperclassman did the same for me once when I was breaking in as a Hot Pilot. By the way, Mr. Davis, I want to commend you for the fine job you did cleaning up that coffee you spilled. I'm sure it won't happen again, because, you see, it simply takes more time away from your eating—time which you don't have too much of, because of your duties as Hot Pilot. Right, Mr. Davis?"

"Yes, sir." Seething inside, Neal gobbled his rice pudding and found it soothing.

Cement Face watched, smiling. "We hate to interrupt, Mr. Davis. But could you sit up just a little straighter? That's it—shoulders back, chin in. That's splendid."

"Yes, sir." And to himself Neal said, I'd like to take what's left of this rice pudding and ram it right into that insolent face. Oh no, you don't, warned an inner voice. Control yourself. Obey, give in—on the surface at least. And wasn't it nice of Mr. Blackstone to let you eat your rice pudding? Nice? Neal answered himself, outraged. Nice? It was salt poured on the wound, that's what it was. Nevertheless, not even Cement Face and his diabolical brainwashing could completely spoil the delicious taste of the rice pudding.

"Finished, Mr. Davis? Fine. A little straighter now, please. That's it. And Hot Pilot, just one more cup of coffee for my good friend, Mr. Willoughby."

"Yes, sir," said Neal. As he poured and passed without spilling, he said to himself, Corn Pone has now had about ten cups of coffee. I hope it keeps the clown awake all night.

CHAPTER 10

The doolies were back in their room in Vandenberg Hall. The Yankee had his tool kit out, and was removing the adjustable screw driver.

"Imagine not letting me wiggle my ears," he protested. "This is more tyrannical than Portland Prep." He sighed. "But we must fight, Davis. We have lost a battle but not the war. Remember Concord and Lexington, Ticonderoga and Trenton."

Neal was slumped in his chair. "And Waterloo," he added.

"Do not despair," said the Yankee. "See this?" He had taken another object out of his suitcase, a square object with an electric cord. "Know what it is?"

Neal yawned. He was tired, still somewhat hungry, and rather skeptical of the Yankee's strategy. After all, hadn't he had his ears pinned back at the dining table? "I suppose it's a bomb," he said sarcastically, "but it looks like an electric clock."

116

"Right," said the Yankee. Placing the clock on his desk, he deftly removed its back and exposed its works. "See this?" he said, pointing with his screw driver.

"Not from here," said Neal. But he got up with a grunt and crossed the room to look. "Uh huh," he said. "Looks like a gear of some kind."

"It's my special ratchet wheel," said the Yankee. "See those notches in the wheel? When the gizmo hits the notches, it releases the bell system and rings the alarm."

"Oh," said Neal.

"It can ring the alarm several times," said the Yankee proudly. "The average electric clock rings only once."

"Ah," said Neal.

The Yankee made his conspiratorial gesture, finger against nose. "Are you ready to enlist in the Resistance, Davis?"

Neal grinned. "It depends on the terms."

"Simple terms," said the Yankee. "I plan the strategy, you carry it out."

"Oh," said Neal, "I get it. In other words, I'm the guy who goes on the dangerous mission."

"It's the way of all resistance movements, Davis," said the Yankee. "The Brain, overworked at headquarters, has a nervous breakdown. The Brawn gets wounded in the field."

"Uh huh," said Neal. "O.K., explain my mission."

"Sure," said the Yankee. "But first let me put away

the tools of my dangerous trade, in case the secret police descend upon us unexpectedly." As he put his weapons away, the Yankee murmured, "Hiding place for tool kit—false bottom in the clothes hamper. Priority A. Agreed, Davis?"

"O.K. by me," said Neal. It was undoubtedly a good idea to hide anything extracurricular from the snooping eyes of Corn Pone and Cement Face. No doubt about it, the Yankee was shrewd, though slightly insane. Perhaps it was just the kind of personality needed to combat this tyranny. Neal listened with greater interest to a description of his "dangerous mission."

"It's all based on psychology," whispered the Yankee, after glancing over his shoulder. "Tomorrow morning and every morning thereafter, except Sundays, the bugle will blow reveille over the PA system at 5:55 A.M."

"I was afraid of that," sighed Neal.

"A gruesomely early hour," said the Yankee. "We'll wait a few days, let the schedule get underway, and play it cool with Corn Pone and Cement Face. We'll pretend they've got us licked—we've bowed under, become obedient slaves. And then—we strike!" The ears wiggled, the eyes flickered.

"How?" said Neal, and this time he was rather tense, because he knew that he was the striking force.

"The bomb goes off in their room," said Ethan Hoyt bluntly.

"The bomb?" said Neal nervously.

"The electric alarm," said the Yankee. "Look." He beckoned and led the way to the lavatory. Neal followed. The Yankee was pointing to the vent near the clothes hamper. "Once you get into their lavatory, you unscrew this plate and put the clock inside. Conceal the wire by running it behind the hamper, and plug it in here." He pointed to the electrical outlet. "Simple?"

"Sort of," said Neal. "But I'm not as fast with that screw driver as you are, Hoyt."

"You will be after practice," said the Yankee.

"O.K.," said Neal. "But what happens when the alarm goes off? It wakes 'em up. Sure, that's fine. But they get up, trace the noise to its source, and pull out the plug."

"Oh no," said the Yankee. "That's where the psychology comes in. They don't wake up thinking clearly. They wake up groggy, their subconscious struggling. When they wake up like that, they don't jump out of bed and rush at the noise—not after a tough day at the Academy. They lie there half-asleep. BRRING. The bell continues. By the time they decide to do something about it, it stops. So they go back to sleep."

"Oh," said Neal, testing the theory out on himself. It sounded reasonable.

"That's 1 A.M.," said the Yankee. "Two hours later,

when they're sound asleep again, it goes off the second time. BRRING. Slowly they come out of their subconscious. Is it their alarm clock? 'You check it,' says Corn Pone. 'You check it,' says Cement Face. They argue."

"Wait a minute," said Neal. "Suppose they don't have an alarm clock."

"Everyone here has an alarm clock," said the Yankee. "Why? Because reveille is so early. The bugle blows at 5:55. You wake up, and then go back to sleep. Your alarm goes off at 6. You wake up and hustle, or you miss formation at 6:15."

"I'll accept it," said Neal. "O.K., they lie there in bed and argue and finally decide that it's not their alarm clock that's ringing—that blasted noise is coming from their lavatory."

"Wrong," said the Yankee. "Remember, they're still groggy. Why should a noise like that come from a lavatory? It must be coming from the room next door. Besides, by this time it's stopped. The gizmo on my special ratchet wheel is designed to keep the armature vibrating just long enough to make the alarm bell as maddening as the buzzing of a mosquito. It flies in and wakes them up. They swat at it. It flies away, and they go back to sleep. Then it buzz bombs them again."

"I get it," said Neal, with growing enthusiasm. "Then what?"

"Then this," said the Yankee. "At 5 A.M. their own alarm goes off."

"*Their* alarm?" said Neal, surprised.

"That's step two in your mission," said the Yankee sternly. "You plant my alarm in the vent, and then you set theirs for five instead of six."

"But won't they notice it?" said Neal.

"I doubt it," said the Yankee. "They never did at Portland Prep. Most clowns set their alarm for the same time every morning, and leave it. In other words, they don't worry about the pointer on the little dial; they worry only about the plunger that starts the electric cycle. They pull out the plunger at night and push it in, comes morning. After the first four or five nights they assume that their clock is still set for six—five minutes after reveille. Right?"

"Possibly," said Neal, nodding.

"BRRING," said the Yankee. "At five o'clock the mosquito strikes again. Where is that infernal noise coming from? This time they're mad as hornets. They get up and trace the noise. It's coming from their alarm clock! It's time to get up. What happens next?"

Hoyt threw up his bony hands. "Anything, Davis, anything. Let's let them figure it out—it's their problem. Right?" The Yankee smiled craftily, and cracked his knuckles contentedly.

"I hope so," said Neal.

The Yankee was laying his finger against his nose.

"How about it, Davis? Now that you've heard the plan, will you enlist, become a member of the Resistance, fight the good fight?"

Neal took a deep breath. "O.K.," he said. "Count me in. I have only two questions. I plant your alarm clock in the vent and plug it in. I sabotage their alarm clock—set it an hour early. Then is my mission over?"

"Yes, Davis," said the Yankee. "You may then consider your mission accomplished."

"Good," said Neal. "Let's shake hands on that." They shook hands solemnly, and then he said with a grin, "Now for the second question. Who goes back in their room the next day and retrieves your alarm clock? You?" I've got him there, reflected Neal. He's thought of everything except that one important detail.

But the Yankee wasn't surprised or flustered. "The Resistance," he said. "No names. No link in the chain of conspiracy should know the name of the next link, in case of capture and torture. Our new agent is a doolie two rooms down the hall from Corn Pone and Cement Face. The next day, when the upperclassmen are absent, this brave doolie, armed with my screw driver, will carry out his mission and retrieve the alarm clock."

Neal's curiosity was deepened by the Yankee's dramatization. "I think I should know who my fellow agent is," he said.

"As a matter of fact," the Yankee admitted, "I haven't signed him up yet. But he'll do it, don't worry. He's unhappy and resentful. He was a big shot in high school, and now he's just another doolie."

"Ah," said Neal. "Dell Hubbard."

Suddenly Ethan's ears were cocked, his voice was a hoarse whisper. "They're coming!"

"Not again!" cried Neal. "Can't they ever leave us alone?"

The Yankee smiled grimly. "We fascinate them, Davis."

"Obviously," said Neal.

"At-ten-SHUN!" Cement Face cracked the command. He and Corn Pone were now wearing blue bathrobes, decorated with bogus medals for bad conduct, punishment tours, and general derelictions. They looked less severe than in uniform, but their words belied their appearance.

"All right, mister, get those shoulders back. Back! And suck in that stomach. I said suck it in!"

Neal braced his shoulders, pulled in his stomach, and seethed inside. The Yankee was absolutely right. This was war, total war. Neal was glad now that he had enlisted in the Yankee's Underground, and he was sure that Dell Hubbard, the high-school hero reduced to zero, would feel the same. Working for the mastermind, Ethan Hoyt, they would successfully rebel against the tyrants. Otherwise, as the Yankee had warned, their personalities would certainly perish under this continued brainwashing.

"Mr. Hoyt." Corn Pone was circling the Yankee. "Ah want to say your posture has improved one hundred per cent. Don't you agree, Mr. Blackstone?"

"Yes indeed, Mr. Willoughby."

As Corn Pone circled his victim, Neal spotted a Confederate flag, sewn on the back of the southerner's bathrobe. Corn Pone was saying, "Ah notice, too, that your ears have also learned to stand at attention, Mr. Hoyt. That's better. There's no place at the Academy for wigglin' ears—it isn't dignified."

"No, sir," said the Yankee.

If they only knew, thought Neal. They think the Yankee's surrendered. They'll find out—the clowns.

Cement Face smiled. "Yes, Mr. Willoughby, I agree. There's been a great improvement in both of these doolies. I think they're ready for their exams now."

Exams, thought Neal. We haven't even been told what to study.

"Mr. Davis," said Cement Face sternly, "what is a doolie?"

"A fourth classman, sir," said Neal.

"Define a doolie, Mr. Davis."

Define a doolie? Neal thought it over. What should he say? A doolie is a dumbbell for standing here and taking it? He decided to stall and say nothing.

"Very well," said Cement Face. "I'll define it for

you. 'A doolie is one whose potential for learning is unlimited.' Repeat that, Mr. Davis."

"A doolie," said Neal, "is one whose—uh—potential for learning is—uh—unlimited."

"Good," said Cement Face. "That is the official definition of a doolie. Tomorrow I want you to be able to rattle it right off. Got it?"

"Yes, sir."

"Are you familiar with *Contrails,* Mr. Davis?"

"Yes, sir," said Neal. "It's the cadet handbook."

"That's correct, Mr. Davis. But now I want the scientific definition of contrails."

Neal was glad he knew it. "Condensation trails, sir," he said.

"That's partly correct, mister," said Cement Face. "But tomorrow I want you to be ready with this definition: 'Contrails—a visible trail of water droplets or ice crystals, formed in the wake of an aircraft, flying at high altitude.' Got it, Mr. Davis?"

"Yes, sir."

Cement Face continued relentlessly. "In addition, Mr. Davis, I want you to memorize from the cadet handbook the objectives of the Air Force Academy. Got that?"

"Yes, sir," said Neal. He got it all right. Gadzooks!

Corn Pone took over. "Mr. Hoyt! To what school do we refer when we say Hudson High?"

The Yankee thought for a moment, and then answered, "West Point."

Corn Pone was taken aback. He glanced at his ally. "How about that, Mr. Blackstone? The Yankee guessed it. Can you define Hudson High, Mr. Hoyt?" asked Corn Pone.

"No, sir."

"A-ha!" said Corn Pone. "Then be ready tomorrow with this definition: 'West Point is a little school on the Hudson River, having 156 years of tradition unhampered by progress.' Got it, Mr. Hoyt?"

"I think so, sir."

"Repeat it, mister."

The Yankee repeated it.

"Good," said Corn Pone. "Ah assume that you, too, have your copy of *Contrails*. Your first assignment in it will be to memorize the Honor Code. Got that, mister?"

"Yes, sir."

Cement Face took over again. "All right, Mr. Davis, your turn. To what school do we refer when we say Canoe U?"

Neal thought it over, remembering the Yankee's answer. If Hudson High was West Point, then Canoe U must be—"Annapolis," he said.

"Right!" said Cement Face. He smiled at his ally. "How about that, Mr. Willoughby? My boy is bright, too."

"Most promisin'," said Corn Pone.

"I agree," said Cement Face. "Too bad we can't work on these two doolies all summer."

"A doggone shame," said Corn Pone. "But they must have their trainin' in the field, Mr. Blackstone. There's nothin' like a forced march on a broilin'-hot road with an M-1 rifle on your achin' shoulder and a full pack on your achin' back. They'll miss our encouragin' words then, Mr. Blackstone."

"Indeed they will," said Cement Face. "Well, gentlemen doolies"—he smiled benevolently—"we shall now bid you good night, so you can get to your memory work. From the brilliant answers you've already given, I'm sure that the simple work assigned for tonight will give you no trouble. And tomorrow there will be more assignments, won't there, Mr. Willoughby?"

"Yes, indeedy," said Corn Pone. "Ah'm sure they'll look forward to memorizin'—in addition to the Honor Code and the objectives of the Air Force Academy— the History of the U. S. Air Force, insignia of rank, U. S. Air Force aircraft and missile designations, military decorations, and so on."

"And so on and so on," said Cement Face with a smile. "Good night, gentlemen. Study hard."

They left. The Yankee waited until they were out of earshot and then let out a groan. "I hate memory work," he said. "I don't even like to read." He slouched to his desk, picked up his copy of *Contrails*, and flopped in his chair. "The Honor Code," he mumbled. "I'm getting into one of my black moods."

"What are *they* like?" said Neal. The wildly imaginative, slightly maniacal moods were difficult enough—the black moods might be dangerous.

"Gloom," said the Yankee. "It's creeping over me like a huge black shadow." He shivered. "Those guys are getting me down, Davis. They're finally getting to me."

"Maybe you're just tired," said Neal. "When you get tired you feel low. I do sometimes."

"I suppose that's right," said the Yankee. He sighed. "You were an athlete at high school, weren't you, Davis?"

"More or less," said Neal. "I played football and tennis."

"Competitive sports," sighed the Yankee. "They teach you to compete, to fight on, to persevere—that sort of thing. It's corny but highly useful."

"I agree," said Neal. He was thinking of the perseverance that had carried him through the arduous training for the Academy exams.

"I can see," said the Yankee glumly, "that you've got some of that old do-or-die spirit, Davis. I even have it myself sometimes. But not often enough. Cross-country was my only sport at Portland Prep." The Yankee had sunk deep in his chair, his chin on his chest. "It was crazy, that cross-country. Fifty guys in a three-mile rat race over stone walls and through poison ivy. What a circus! I finally had to quit, Davis. *You* wouldn't have quit."

"Oh, I might have," said Neal. But would I have? he asked himself. He was remembering a moment in the Thanksgiving Day game, when he had been tempted to quit. He hadn't, and had saved the day.

"I wasn't much of an athlete," said the Yankee. "But I was a whiz at math and physics. I guess that's what got me in here, plus the fact that I come from Maine, where the competition for an appointment is nothing, compared to California." The Yankee smiled thinly. "Incidentally, I was also a member of the Portland Prep debating team and the Bird-Watching Society."

"The what?" said Neal.

"Bird watching," said the Yankee. "I won a prize one year for spotting the first robin. How about that, Davis?"

"Fine," said Neal. He could have kidded Ethan Hoyt about bird watching, but it didn't seem right somehow. The Yankee looked too gloomy and vulnerable.

"Want to know one of the minor reasons I'm here?" said the Yankee. "It sounds crazy, but here it is. The mascot of this joint is the falcon—a bird of prey. West Point has a mule as mascot, the Navy has a goat, but the Air Force Academy has a falcon—a bird. I think it's wonderful, Davis. It's one of the reasons I'm here."

"I see," said Neal. He did see—in a way. The Yankee was as mad as a hatter, but he was mad in an interesting way.

Thinking of the falcons seemed to have lifted Hoyt out of his gloom for a moment. "They train falcons here, Davis. Think of the fun that would be. How would you like to be a falconer, Davis?"

"It never occurred to me," said Neal.

"Well, it's occurred to me," said the Yankee. He sighed, and fell silent and glum again. Disdainfully thumbing his copy of *Contrails,* he read aloud in a forlorn voice, " 'The Honor Code.' " He wagged his head. "I don't think I can do it, Davis. I hate memory work."

"You can do it," said Neal. "Look, you read it over, and then I'll test you on it, sentence by sentence. You'll be surprised how easy it is when two work on it."

"O.K." said the Yankee. "Do or die." In a funereal voice he began reading. " 'We will not lie, cheat, or steal, nor tolerate among us anyone who does.' " The Yankee stopped and sighed. "It's difficult, Davis, difficult. A stern code—hard to memorize, hard to live up to. But we can be thankful for one thing."

"What's that?" said Neal.

The Yankee managed a wan smile. "It says nothing about monkeying with the wiring."

############ *CHAPTER 11* ############

Tock-tack, tocka-tack. Tock-tack, tocka-tack.

The noise forced its way into Neal's dreams. A Colorado woodpecker was batting his beak against the picture window.

The Yankee was annoyed. "I'm going to shoot that little son of a gun," he said.

Neal protested. "You can't do that. You're an ex-member of the Portland Prep Bird-Watching Society. Bird watchers don't shoot. . . ."

Bom-bam, bomba-bam. The gun went off. The Mad Yankee was firing a Browning automatic. The noise nudged Neal up and out of another woolly layer of sleep. He woke up and heard the last bugle notes of reveille, "Gotta get up this morning."

He struggled to get up, failed, and slipped back to sleep.

BRRING. A jackhammer was bearing down on

him. BRRINNG. It was the electric alarm clock, stir-
ring the voice of conscience. Don't let yourself go back
to sleep. This is your last chance. Get up!

He got up, staggered to the lavatory, dashed cold
water on his face, and woke up completely.

Ethan Hoyt was still in the sack, sound asleep. Neal
shook him gently. "Beat it," muttered the Yankee, and
turned over. Neal shook him again, less gently. "Get
lost!" grunted the Yankee.

Neal gave him a real shake, and the Yankee came up
swinging, with a roundhouse right. Neal blocked the
blow, delivered a short but pithy opinion of such belligerent ingratitude and, pulling the Yankee out of
the sack, dumped him on the floor. Still only half-
awake, the Yankee struggled to his feet, swinging
wildly and releasing a torrent of delirious abuse aimed
at the Academy, Corn Pone, Cement Face, and Neal
Davis.

Neal went in under the fists with a driving tackle
that deposited the Yankee on his bed and brought him
almost completely to his senses. "Hey!" he cried.
"What's going on here? I didn't go out for football."

"Get up!" Neal commanded.

The Yankee groaned. "I can't, Davis. They've done
me in. They've won, Davis. I'm through."

"On your feet!" said Neal, pulling the Yankee to a
sitting position. "We're going to take a shower."

"I've had it," said the Yankee, swaying.

"Let's go!" said Neal. "The Resistance can't afford to lose its mastermind."

"You carry on, Davis," said the Yankee. "I resign," and so saying, he fell back into bed.

Not for long. A glass of ice-cold Colorado mountain water smacked him full in the face. He sat up and again jumped to his feet, swinging and swearing, only to find himself hustled off to the showers, where he became completely conscious and clearheaded. "Brr! Help! All right! O.K.! I'm awake! You can turn on the warm water now, Davis, please!"

Gradually, under the benign influence of the shower, the Yankee became grateful and contrite. "I said you were the do-or-die type, Davis. I spotted that streak of perseverance in you."

"Someone has to put this show on the road," said Neal. "We can't miss formation and breakfast. Corn Pone and Cement Face would never let us forget it."

"You're right, Davis," said the Yankee, drying himself. "I'm sorry I was so slow coming out of my subconscious. But you see, it proves my point. When you go to sleep here, you really go down deep. Waking up is like coming out of an anesthetic. So much the better for the Resistance, Davis, with Operation Alarm Clock."

"Hot Pilot!"

"Yes, sir."

"One coffee down the ramp!"

"Cold Pilot!"

"Yes, sir."

"Two milks! Fly 'em down!"

"Mr. Davis, define a doolie."

"A doolie, sir," said Neal, "is one whose potential for learning is unlimited."

"Mr. Hoyt, ah want you to define Hudson High."

"Hudson High, sir, is a little school on the Hudson River, having 156 years of tradition unhampered by progress."

Harassed at every turn, hustled from one duty to the next, they still managed to plot and plan for Operation Alarm Clock. Dell Hubbard—"Doolie Dell," as he was now called—was recruited by the Yankee as the second secret agent. While Corn Pone and Cement Face bowled after dinner in the alleys at Arnold Hall, the three conspirators rehearsed their act of sabotage, using Doolie Dell's room as their base of operations. The Yankee was a perfectionist, and his agents became impatient. When was H hour, D day?

The Yankee set a date, then postponed it. Was he losing his nerve? He denied it indignantly. He was thinking, he claimed, of the welfare of his agents. Suppose they were caught. The enemies would have less time for reprisals if Operation Alarm Clock went off shortly before the doolies' day of departure for their training in the field.

Finally, three days before the doolies were to leave Vandenberg Hall, Ethan Hoyt gave the word—D day was at hand.

Down the long hall that evening went Neal Davis on his dangerous mission, the "secret weapon" concealed inside a bath towel. Neal, if stopped, was to say he was on his way to the showers. Stationed at the head of a spiral staircase stood secret agent Doolie Dell. By an almost imperceptible nod of his tonsured head, he gave the signal, the coast was clear.

Without changing his pace, Neal slipped into the room shared by Cement Face and Corn Pone, and stood still, staring. Here it was, the sanctum sanctorum, the home base of the tyrants. There were the desks and beds and books, as neatly arranged as objects in a store-window display. It was extremely tempting. He had to fight off a strong impulse to wreck this silent symbol of tyranny and order. He longed to strip the beds, overturn the tables, hurl the books and chairs out the window.

Suppressing the impulse, he proceeded to a more subtle type of revenge. First, to set the tyrants' own alarm clock. He found it set, as expected, for 6 A.M., five minutes after reveille. Quickly but carefully Neal reset it for 5 A.M. Then he started on the second step of his mission.

In the lavatory waited the electrical outlet, the clothes hamper, and the vent. Neal's fingers were moist with nervous perspiration, but diligent practice with the screw driver had greatly improved his manual dexterity. Off the vent came the grilled plate. In went the electrical alarm clock, its special wheel set by Ethan Hoyt for 1 A.M. and 3 A.M. Concealing the cord by running it behind the clothes hamper, Neal connected the clock to the electrical outlet. All was ready.

He checked it again to make sure. The plug was in tight, the cord was well concealed as it disappeared through the grill of the vent. Only a sharp investigation in bright light would detect it—not a sleepy search in the dark. Check and double check. It was time to go.

Suddenly there screamed like a siren, on hearing hypersensitive because of tension, the sound of two low whistles—the warning signal from Doolie Dell—they're coming!

Impossible! He couldn't have taken that long. They must have decided not to go bowling in Arnold Hall. No matter. Scram!

He fled, and in his flight forgot the towel in which the clock had been wrapped. He had left the telltale towel in the lavatory, where it might well arouse suspicion. He had to fight off panic, double back in his tracks, and sweep up the towel, as if recovering a fumble on a football field.

Heart pounding, he reached the corridor and glanced toward the staircase. Doolie Dell had vanished, but the heads of the enemy were not yet visible. Then suddenly up the staircase floated the southern accent of Corn Pone. Usually it had an irritating effect. Now it sounded sinister—all the more sinister, because it was conversing casually.

For a split second Neal froze. Then he took off down the long corridor, his heart racing faster than his feet. Perfect timing and great self-control were needed here, just as in a broken-field run. He had to get far enough away to escape detection, but if he went too fast he would arouse suspicion. At any moment he expected to hear the dreaded call, signifying that the jig was up—"Just a cotton-pickin' minute, Mr. Davis." The call did not come; he had not been identified. He went on, breathing more normally. But he was still tense when he reached his room far down the hall.

Ethan Hoyt was pacing the floor, hands behind his back. He stopped and stood still, his antenna ears tuned in for the news, good or bad. "Did you make it, Davis?"

Neal nodded, let out a sigh, and slumped into a chair. He felt as if he had just run back a kickoff for a touchdown. "By the skin of my teeth," he said.

"Well done, Davis," said the Yankee. "You'll get the Air Medal for this."

"Nuts with the Air Medal," said Neal. "Just give me a glass of water and some smelling salts."

Secret agent Doolie Dell turned in his report later.

Corn Pone had unexpectedly returned, simply because he had forgotten his special bowling shoes. Doolie Dell had heard him say as much to another upperclassman. "Ah just plumb forgot mah shoes."

"He would," said the Yankee. "Were his suspicions aroused?"

"Not at all," said Doolie Dell.

"Fine," said the Yankee, cracking his knuckles. "So far, so good."

At 12:55 A.M. absolute silence reigned in Vandenberg Hall. Everyone was sleeping the deep sleep of exhaustion, brought on by the relentless Academy schedule and the clear, cool Colorado mountain air. Twelve-fifty-five A.M. on D day—five minutes before H hour. Utter silence, deep sleep—except for three doolies, Neal Davis, Ethan Hoyt, and Dell Hubbard.

The Yankee was staring at the phosphorus hands on his wrist watch, ticking off the time. "Two minutes," he whispered. "Now one minute and forty-five seconds . . . thirty seconds . . . twenty . . . five. One-two-three-four—"

BRRING!

The bell was faint and distant, but distinctly audible in the deep, dark quiet. The Yankee let out a hoarse triumphant whisper. "You did it, Davis, you did it! You'll get the Distinguished Flying Cross!"

"Thank you," said Neal. His thanks were only slightly sardonic; his delight was very real indeed. "I wish we were nearer," he whispered. "I'd like to hear what those two clowns are saying."

Silence reigned again in Vandenberg Hall—deep heavy silence. It was 2 A.M., 2:30, 2:55, 2:59.

BRRINNG!

Far down the corridor the Yankee exulted. "We did it again, Davis! I'll see that you get the Medal of Honor for this!"

"Get one for yourself while you're at it," said Neal, chuckling.

"And another thing," said the Yankee. "I think the time has finally come for us to be on a first-name basis. Great work, Neal. Shake!"

Neal grinned as he shook hands, and said, "Thank you, Ethan." It was an odd name, Ethan, and a strange ceremony. And yet, because of the circumstances, there was something more than sardonic about it. Using last names through an ordeal made the use of first names after it rather impressive.

Silence fell again. At 4 A.M. the silence was very deep—at 4:30, the same—4:55, still the same—5. BRRINNNGGG! A loud, long, and insistent brring!

From the victims' room rose mumbles, grunts, curses. From the suffering upperclassmen next to the victims' room, angry squawks. "Knock it off, you fatheads!" "What are you running in there—a repair shop for alarm clocks?" "Turn that blasted thing off!"

At 5:55 A.M. the bugle sounded reveille. Cement

Face and Corn Pone woke up, groaned, and went back to sleep. At 6 their clock was supposed to go off. It didn't. In all the nocturnal noise and confusion they had forgotten to reset it.

At 6:30 hunger pangs woke up Corn Pone. Frantically he and Cement Face dressed, and rushed to the dining hall. They were not only tired and cranky from the sleep they had lost—they were fearful, because they had missed formation. Absent that morning was their usual conversation, calculated to get under the doolies' skin. Commands to the Hot and Cold Pilots were confined to actual needs; there were no requests for special services. Nor did the upperclassmen seem interested even in talking to each other. Their semisilence was sullen, and their conversation consisted chiefly of grunts and monosyllables, interspersed with stifled yawns.

As for the doolies, Neal Davis and Ethan Hoyt, they played it cool, quietly concealing their jubilation. When Corn Pone groaned and yawned, they laughed— but inwardly. When Cement Face grumbled, "What a night that was!" the doolies pretended that the significance of his remark was beyond them, and calmly went about their business, sitting up straight on the edges of their chairs, speaking only when spoken to, and passing the hot and cold drinks. It was one of the quietest celebrations of a major victory in the history of the war—the almost interminable war between doolies and upperclassmen.

IIIIIIIIIIIIIIIIIIIII *CHAPTER 12* IIIIIIIIIIIIIIIIIIIII

"Hup-two-three-four!"

They were marching down a Colorado road with full packs on their backs and M-1 rifles on their shoulders. It was cool and clear in the early morning, the doolies were rested, and the regular army officers kept the discipline impersonal.

"This is the life," said Neal. "Just inhale that clean mountain air, Ethan. Smell that sage, smell that pine!"

"Uh-huh," said the Yankee.

"I thought you were a nature lover," kidded Neal.

"I'm a bird watcher," said the Yankee. "There's a difference."

"O.K.," said Neal. "Look! There's a blue jay perched on that pine tree."

"I never did like blue jays," said the Yankee.

Neal chuckled. "You sound gloomy, Ethan."

"I don't like marching," said the Yankee. "I'm allergic to full packs and rifles."

"Look at the bright side of life," said Neal. "Would

141

you rather be back in Vandenberg Hall being braced by Corn Pone and Cement Face?"

The Yankee sighed. "No," he said, "I guess I wouldn't."

Hup-two-three-four!

It was a main road, paved and straight. Then it turned into a dirt road that wound its way up a mountain, and it became hot and dry and dusty—very hot, very dry, and very dusty. The rifles on their shoulders grew hotter and heavier. The straps on their packs cut into sore and aching muscles. The thin mountain air made their breath come in gasps.

Doolie Dell Hubbard was doing all right, but the Yankee was beginning to groan and grunt as he toiled upward. "What are we supposed to be—mountain troops?" He scuffed and stumbled. "I think I'll fall out, Neal. I've had it."

Neal gave him a friendly shove. "Onward and upward, Ethan, for dear old Portland Prep."

Beads of sweat turned into pools, which overflowed and ran down, like rivulets coursing down a dirt slope, through the dust that powdered their faces. The rifles began to burn, the pack straps stung.

The Yankee weaved and swayed. "This is it, Neal. So long, buddy. Carry on."

Another friendly shove helped him upward. "Just get to the top of this rise, Ethan, and you've got it made."

Neal didn't know what was at the top of the rise or whether getting to it would make any difference, but he wanted to give the Yankee a visible objective instead of an agonizingly indefinite goal.

Groaning and grunting, the Yankee reached the top of the rise.

"See!" Neal exclaimed, with a note of triumph.

They found themselves on an open grassy plateau, which was several miles wide. At the other end gleamed the inviting water of a mountain lake. To Neal it was a beautiful and inspiring sight, but the Yankee derived no inspiration from it. "O.K.," he mumbled, "I made it. Now I fall out."

"Fall out!" The echo was a coincidental command from one of the officers in charge of the march. "Ten-minute break!"

Ethan Hoyt flopped on the grass. Neal sat down, unscrewed the top of his canteen, and gave his companion a drink. Ten minutes later, when the doolies resumed their march, the Yankee went with them, revived by the rest and continually prodded from the rear—verbally or physically. Fortunately the marching was easier now. It was level and cooler, and the water of the mountain lake beckoned like the friendly palms of a desert oasis.

Later they pitched camp near the lake, and plunged into its clear but icy water. Supper was served in mess kits. They were ravenously hungry, and hot dogs and baked beans tasted just as good as steak and French fries.

The night was cold, and the stars were clear and close under the Colorado sky. Neal and the Yankee shared a tent, and Dell Hubbard joined them. Dell asked, "How do you feel, Ethan?"

"Exhausted," said the Yankee. "I didn't think I signed up for the infantry. I thought I joined the Air Force."

"We just got shot down over enemy territory," said Neal.

Dell Hubbard laughed, but the Yankee groaned. "I wonder if I'll make it tomorrow."

"You made it today," said Neal, "so your chances of making it tomorow are better."

Another grunt. "Do or die, I suppose," said the Yankee.

"The power of positive thinking," said Neal.

"Uh-huh."

"Pleasant hikes in the Colorado mountains," said Neal. "Summer camp in the Rockies. People pay good money for this privilege, Ethan."

"Yeah?" said the Yankee. "And they also have sure-footed friends to carry their guns and packs—they have mules."

"That kind of camper is soft," said Neal. "We're being toughened up."

"For what?" said the Yankee.

"For fall sports," said Dell Hubbard. "For soccer—that's my game."

"For football," said Neal.

"I don't play either one," said the Yankee glumly. "What have I got to look forward to?"

Neal suddenly remembered. "To falconry," he said.

"Falconry!" cried the Yankee. "Of course. I was so pooped I forgot the finest bird of all—the falcon. I hope I make falconer."

"You will," said Neal. "You're as nuts about falconry as I am about football."

The training in the field ended, and the instructors gave the survivors a reward—a visit to an Air Force base and a flight in a jet. This was the life, thought Neal, as he soared up into the wild blue yonder. It was indeed, but it ended all too quickly. In September he was back at the Academy being handed a stack of books. The stack was so high that he found it hard to believe they were all for him.

Studies were rushing at Neal like enemy tacklers rushing downfield after a kickoff. This game of English, history, and math was complicated, and the rules of the Honor Code, by which it was played, were difficult. The most difficult part about the code was that you had to apply it yourself. You were on your own. The instructor handed you the test questions and then left the classroom, giving you every opportunity to cheat if you were tempted.

It was confusing and, at times, discouraging. But behind the confusion and discouragement there loomed one thing that would make it all worthwhile, freshman football.

Eagerly Neal reported for the freshman team, and was appalled by what he found there. For one thing, the size of that squad! Could all these guys be trying out just for the freshman team? The ability of too many of the candidates was visible even in sweat-suit workouts. There weren't just two standouts here, like Tony Spoldi and Don Latimer—there were many Tony Spoldis and Don Latimers.

"Hup-two-kick! Hup-three-bend!" A trim assistant coach, wearing a baseball cap, was barking the orders. Obediently Neal kicked and bent. Setting-up exercises were boring, but they didn't bother him too much. What bothered him was the size of the squad and the obvious ability of too many of its members—especially the candidates for the backfield. A halfback named Moose Moore and a quarterback named Frank Chandler both looked like varsity material.

It was disheartening. Neal knew that he was bigger and stronger than he had been at Fairview, but he could also tell that he was not in the same class as Chandler and Moore. The question was not simply whether he could work his way up to that class; it also depended on whether he could survive the coaches' cut, which would disqualify half of the squad.

The sweat suits were exchanged for padded uniforms, and the setting-up exercises became long sessions in blocking and tackling. Neal's doubts increased. There were at least twenty-two men on the squad who blocked and tackled better than he did. It would take all his diligence and determination to win a place on the third team, if blocking and tackling counted as much as the coaching emphasis indicated.

Charge! He left his cleats and hurled himself at the blocking dummy. Thump! Down it went, but not crisply enough. Crunch! Cleats churning, he had rammed into the tackling dummy and dragged it down with him. Too much drag and too little punch. It was discouraging.

Nor did his deficiencies escape the eagle eye of the assistant coach. "Get more butt in that block, mister. Get more shoulder in that tackle." The voice barked the commands. Here was no mild-mannered, pink-cheeked coach like Mr. Grigsby, who really preferred baseball. To this grim coach, a captain in the Air Force, football was the only sport that counted, and at the Academy it had to be played by perfectionists.

Time after time, day after day, Neal charged the dummies and knocked them down with blocks and tackles that slowly and painfully improved. Finally he reached a certain degree of competence in these fundamentals. He wasn't sure that it was enough, but he hoped that his ability as a ball carrier would make up the difference. He was big and fast—not the biggest and fastest man on the squad, but big and fast enough for his height and weight. When practice went on to passing, he held his own. His big hands could catch a pass as well as any of the other backs.

But when the first scrimmage was called he didn't get in until it was almost over. Although he ran reasonably well with the ball he couldn't do what he wanted to do—break into the clear and go all the way. He wanted desperately to show these coaches that he was a first-class ball carrier, but he got to carry the ball only twice. The first time there was no opening, and the second time he was hit, and hit hard, after a three-yard gain.

Although it was discouraging, he noticed that his blocking was better on offense, and when his number was called he got one more chance to distinguish himself. It was on an optional pass play. The quarterback could throw to three potential receivers, either of the ends or the left half, Neal Davis. The man who got in the clear at the right time would become the target.

"Hup-two-three—" The quarterback took the ball and faded. Neal faked, slid over the scrimmage line, cut, and dashed into the clear. When he turned, his heart leaped. He had been selected; the pass was being thrown to him! His big hands reached, grabbed the

ball, and got a good grip on it. It was just as well that
they did, for in the next second he was hit so hard he
almost fumbled. He didn't mind the collision. He
had made his first good gain as a Falcon.

But was he a Falcon? This scrimmage had been between the third and fourth teams, not between the
first and second. Forty-four men. And there were still
twice as many as that fighting for positions on the
squad. It was a long, hard, discouraging pull, and there
were times when he didn't think he would make it—
especially after the first scrimmage in which he had
been allowed to play.

He was dead tired, almost exhausted, both mentally
and physically. It was one of those black moments
when everything seemed to be conspiring against him.
There was just one bright spot—that completed pass.
But was that bright enough? Did that come anywhere
near the glory of a great punt runback or the thrill
of a long run around the end—something that would
really make him stand out on that freshman gridiron?

He decided, in his exhaustion and his gloom, that
it was not bright enough. He had reached the end of
his rope. The competition was too tough athletically,
when coupled with the exacting requirements of the
academic program. Something had to give, or he
would crack up, flunk out. And that was a disgrace
that must not happen. Then what? A wise decision

must be made here, using every brain cell that wasn't completely fatigued.

Forcing his brain to an ultimate effort, Neal found the thought he wanted and made the decision—he would give up freshman football. In its place he would substitute a less exacting sport, tennis. By this wise maneuver he was fairly sure he could survive his first semester at the Air Force Academy.

The decision, once made, took a great weight off his shoulders. He was surprised at how relieved he felt. But he was irked by the Yankee's reaction. Although Ethan Hoyt was sometimes sardonic about the do-or-die spirit and "the old college try," he admired them in others. Besides, something else was involved.

"Listen, Neal," he said. "Let's face it. Football is a prestige sport. The very fact that you go out for it improves your standing. And if you have a good chance of making the team, your status goes up another notch."

"Probably," said Neal. "But I think I'll let my status slip this season."

"But what about me?" said the Yankee, with a suspicion of a smile.

"You?" said Neal. "Where do you come in?"

"If I'm the roommate of the football player," said the Yankee, "some of the glamour will rub off on me."

"Oh, yeah?" said Neal. "Well, if some of the hard work rubbed off on you, maybe you'd feel different."

"O.K.," said the Yankee. "I was only half-serious, anyway. It's really none of my business, Neal. If you want to quit, quit."

Neal snapped at him. "I don't like that word *quit*."

"O.K., O.K.," said the Yankee. "I didn't mean it that way."

"Forget it," said Neal curtly.

In the silence that followed, the Yankee went back to his studies, and Neal, deciding on bed, washed up in the lavatory. While he was there, he decided that he had been too touchy. The Yankee's approach to the subject should have been amusing instead of irritating. In his heavy fatigue Neal had forgotten that football actually was a prestige sport, and that it was perfectly plausible for a nonathlete to benefit from the performance of a football-playing roommate. The Yankee, in his New England way, had just been frank and, by being frank, had meant to be helpful.

In a different mood Neal returned to the room to see the Yankee jumping up as an upperclassman came in, an upperclassman with carrot-colored hair, who smiled and said, "At ease." It was the Falcon, Paul Gregson.

As the Yankee had theorized, Cadet Gregson had traded his summer leave for a tour of air bases in Europe. He talked enthusiastically about people as well as planes. In Paris he had met an Academy graduate, who was studying at the French Air Force school.

In England he had met another graduate, who had won a Rhodes scholarship at Oxford University.

As Cadet Gregson talked, new vistas opened in Neal's imagination. If he made the grade here, he could take one of those wonderful European tours. Those places seemed far, far away, but jets had brought them conveniently near. Neal's imagination, fired up by mental rocket fuel, was blasting off across the Atlantic. But Cadet Gregson brought it quickly back by switching the conversation to a down-to-earth subject—football. "How do you find Falcon football, Neal?"

It was a startling question. It affected Neal in much the same way that the sound of an Air Force jet had once affected him on a beach in southern California. It struck him at a time when he was still mulling over, in the back of his mind, what was the right thing to do.

The Yankee had used the word *quit*, and had withdrawn it when snapped at. He shouldn't have withdrawn it, Neal thought; it was the right word—*quit*. It was a word that couldn't be used in front of Paul Gregson. Why, Gregson was the cadet who had once said at a high-school dance, "You played like a Falcon— for those final few minutes." To quit would be to confirm the implication behind that remark.

They were waiting for the answer, Paul Gregson and Ethan Hoyt. With a wan smile and a warning look at the Yankee, Neal said, "I find Falcon football rough. But I'm still in there."

"Good," said Cadet Gregson.

The Yankee said nothing. Later, when Gregson had gone, Neal thanked Ethan Hoyt for his discreet silence.

The Yankee smiled, the way he always did—thinly. "You don't have to thank me, Neal. Football is a prestige sport, remember? Roommates share some of that prestige."

Still later, Neal tossed restlessly back and forth in bed. Why, he thought, I'll bet Gregson was surprised to see me still here! But I qualified for this Falcon factory, didn't I? Well, here comes another challenge. And I'll do it, he vowed. I'll stay on that freshman squad if I have to carry the water bucket to do it.

CHAPTER 13

Hup-two-kick! Hup-two-bend! He was still trying out for the team. Run lower now, drive, drive! Thump. He hit the blocking dummy. Better, a little better. Get down, stay under that straight-arm! Thump. He hit the tackling dummy. Better, much better. Keep it up, stay in there, keep trying.

One day the list went up on the bulletin board in the locker room, the list of those freshman football players who had survived the cut. Neal was afraid to look. He doubted if his name would be on it. There were too many other good backs, like Moose Moore and Frank Chandler. They didn't even have to look at the list; they knew they were on it.

Perhaps, he thought, he should simply get dressed and sidle out the door, taking his dismissal for granted. It was a temptation, but he didn't give in to it. He got up his nerve, approached the board and, heart thumping anxiously, scanned the alphabetical list. His heart seemed to stop—there was his name! He had made it. Incredible! But then he saw something else after his name, and he knew someone had made a mistake. He had made it as an end, not as a back.

Hurriedly he sought out the assistant coach who had helped him with the blocking and tackling. Anxiously he said, "I was supposed to be a back, sir."

The coach was blunt. "We have plenty of backs, Mr. Davis. We don't have plenty of ends. We are going to convert you from a back to an end."

That was all—terse, blunt, matter-of-fact. Take it or leave it.

Well, he wouldn't take it. He had taken enough. This was too much—the straw that broke the camel's back. All that effort he had put into improving his blocking and tackling had been aimed at qualifying him as a back, not as an end. It was a demotion, no doubt about it. Evidently they, the coaches, did not think he was capable of performing the exciting duties of a back—carrying the ball, running back punts, intercepting passes. Gone forever were those thrilling plays. Now he would be just another drone on the line, blocking and tackling. Did an end ever carry the ball? Rarely. Oh, once in a while they would throw him a pass, like tossing a bone to a stray dog.

He had been fired from the job for which he was so eminently suited. The glory and the excitement had been taken away from him; all the fun had gone out of football. O.K., now he *had* had it; he would turn in his uniform.

And what kind of an impression would that make back at Vandenberg Hall? Not too good a one. They don't play my way, so I'm not going to play at all. That didn't sound so hot. Perhaps he'd better fall back on the other out—football is taking too much of my time; I'd better switch to tennis. But he had tried that one already, and it hadn't worked.

He was in the area now, and he had to trot across it—as if he hadn't done enough running already on the football field! This place was for the birds all right —falcons. And here was good old Vandenberg Hall, with all its glass and aluminum. Spectacular certainly, but cold and unfriendly. Up there behind the picture window would come a conversation that Neal could already hear.

"How'd you make out, Neal?" the Yankee would ask.

"I made it, but as an end, not a back."

"So what? You made it. That's what counts."

"That's what you think, Ethan. You've never played football. You don't know how it feels to be taken out of the backfield and put up in the line."

"Maybe not. But I'd rather play as an end than not at all."

Who said that? Ethan Hoyt? No, Neal Davis, briskly climbing the circular staircase, swinging down the long corridor, and into the room. There was the Yankee, sitting at his desk, turning. Here was the question. "How'd you make out, Neal?"

"I made it," said Neal, and he even managed a wry grin. "But as an end, not as a back."

"Well, what's wrong with being an end?" said the Yankee.

"Nothing," said Neal. "Nothing at all."

He did not believe it at the time, but as the weeks went by he began to find some truth in the statement.

As a lowly left end on the scrubs—but still on the squad—he rushed a passer when the ball was snapped. It wasn't bad, this part of it. It was fairly exciting, like a dash through a dangerous jungle. He bumped off one block and dodged another. Here suddenly was the quarry—the back, trying to pass.

Neal closed in. Jumping, he almost managed to block the pass. He failed in that, but he had the satisfaction of seeing, as he turned, that an alert back on his own fourth team had plucked the hurried pass out of the air. Interception!

But who got all the glamour? The guy who had set up the interception—the end? No—the halfback. Oh, well.

Punt formation. A few plays before, the third team had regained the ball, and they were now going to kick. Dashing in from left end, Neal used all the faking and feinting he had learned as a ball carrier. Working his way through a screen of blockers, he burst in on the kicker. I've got him! Neal exulted. I'll nail him before he gets that punt off.

Without warning, two sounds rang out like rifle shots. The kicker, undeterred by Neal's charge, had booted the ball. Rising sharply and swiftly, it struck Neal in his solar plexus.

He had blocked the kick, but the price he paid was paralyzing. Collapsing, he writhed on the ground, gasping for air that would not come. The shock was deep, the fright intense. He was helpless. He thought his last moments had come.

Instead, there arrived the trainer, brusque and businesslike. Turning Neal over on his back, he loosened his pants, raised his knees, and worked air back into his lungs. In a miraculously short time Neal was breathing normally again. "You just got your wind knocked out, son," said the trainer. "You'll be O.K."

"Sure," said Neal. He spoke carefully, to lighten the burden on his respiratory system. But what he saved on breath he used on mental effort.

Just got my wind knocked out, my eye! I almost got killed. I was just two gasps short of the pearly gates. But never mind. Don't lie here. This isn't the infirmary. Get up and get going. Offer to go back in the game. The offer won't be accepted, but make it anyway. Otherwise, these hard-boiled coaches will think you're chicken.

Taking his own advice, Neal got to his feet. The assistant line coach came up. "O.K., mister?"

"Yes, sir," said Neal. It was a lie, but a brave one. It clued the coach in. He was supposed to say, "All right, Davis, take a seat on the bench for a while."

But the coach apparently had the wrong script. He was saying, "All right, mister, get right back in there. That was a nice blocked kick." And with this compliment the assistant coach gave Neal a pat on the back —a gentle pat out of consideration for his solar plexus.

Neal was taken aback. Nice block indeed! It had laid him flat. But aloud he said, "Thank you, sir." Around here you had to say, "Thank you, sir," even when you got clobbered.

The coach was adding a postscript to his compliment. "The next time you block a kick, mister, do this." The coach crossed his arms in front of his chest, protecting his solar plexus.

"Yes, sir," said Neal.

"Incidentally, mister, you're coming along all right as an end."

"Thank you, sir."

"Now get back in there and fight like a Falcon."

"Yes, sir."

Neal appreciated the coach's compliment, but he

was doubtful about his ever fighting like a Falcon. Every time he tried he seemed to get clobbered. Nevertheless, he remained aware that if it were not for Falcon physical conditioning he wouldn't be able to get back in there at all. Out of his rather groggy memory staggered a mental image of an unpleasant fullback named Fuller, laid low by Cadet Gregson's judo. The cause of the collapse had been similar to Neal's injury. Neal decided, therefore, to forget this accident as quickly as possible—he didn't like its associations. But he was glad that he was able to resume play, when he remembered that fullback Fuller had not been able to resume the fight.

He joined the fourth team in its huddle and was surprised to find himself greeted like an old friend, congratulated, and whacked on the back. He wondered why, and then remembered that he had blocked the kick. The fourth team must have recovered the ball. Although it had been painful, it had also been progress. He wondered how much more he would be able to make and how painful it would be.

Neal was able to make a good deal more progress, and it was increasingly less painful from week to week. As October became November he found himself promoted from the fourth team to the third, and playing almost as well as the second-string end, Joe Mandel, who often got into games as a sub for the first stringer,

Bob Spear. Much of Neal's playing was done on the practice field in scrimmages. On Saturdays he warmed the bench for most of the four periods, while Bob Spear, blond and serious, and Joe Mandel, dark with a bright grin, performed efficiently as first and second stringers.

Neal was definitely a third stringer, but there were several consolations, he told himself. One was that he had survived the cut and made the trips with the squad —for example, up to Denver to play the freshmen of the University of Denver. Secondly, the Academy schedule consumed so much time that there were very few minutes in which a cadet could brood, even if he felt like brooding.

Time flew by like a jet. Suddenly it was Thanksgiving Day, a year after the day of the big game against Greenfield. On this Thanksgiving the big game was against the University of Colorado at Boulder, near Denver.

As Neal changed into his uniform he happened to glance at a mirror. It was one of those rare times when he had a minute to spare. He wasn't hurrying to formation, double timing across the area, or marching to the dining hall. There was no pressure on him athletically, because there were two good men ahead of him, Spear and Mandel. So Neal had time to glance at his reflection, then to do a double-take, to look again, and to stare.

Is that me? Yes, but I look different. How? I dunno —different, older. The shadow of the beard is heavier. The jaw line looks leaner and firmer. The reflection looks taller and broader. Well, it *is*. You've grown another inch and put on more muscle. You're about six foot two now, and you look, perhaps, the way an end ought to look—tall and rangy. You don't mind being an end now, but you started a little too late. Both Bob Spear and Joe Mandel played end at high school and prep school. They had a head start. You've come along pretty fast, but you haven't quite caught up. That's why you're warming the bench here at Boulder.

So he warmed the bench at Boulder, and contemplated the future. His prospects were not too bright. This was a good Falcon freshman team, but the varsity was better. Although two fine left ends, first classmen, were playing their last season for the varsity, two others —third classman Pete Bobko, and second classman Jim Sheridan—would be available next season.

The varsity coach, Ralph Fleet, was undoubtedly getting reports on the performances of the freshmen. He would see that Bob Spear tackled well on defense in these games and that Joe Mandel blocked well on offense. But what would he see about Neal Davis? His record was satisfactory but entirely too slim.

Moreover, in this game against the University of Colorado, the score was tied, 13-13, and subs were being sent in only when absolutely necessary. Joe Mandel had so far played for just a few minutes in the third quarter. Bob Spear's strong defensive play was helping to hold Colorado to short gains on their off-tackle slants and to stop attempts by Colorado for sweeps around their right end.

Now Colorado had the ball on their own thirty-eight, first and ten. They tried to mousetrap Bob Spear on a reverse, but the alert left end held back, fought off a block, and dumped the ball carrier for a three-yard loss. Second and twelve.

A short pass over center was completed, making it third and seven, and then punt formation was called. The blocking was adequate, and the kick carried forty yards to quarterback Frank Chandler, who ran it back ten before being tackled. First and ten, Falcon freshmen on their own thirty-five.

Moose Moore slanted off-tackle for three, a plunge up the middle got two, and then Frank Chandler called a pass play. It was to be a buttonhook pass to Bob Spear. Spear ran down, slanted over toward the center slot, and then cut back sharply, buttonhooking. At this precise moment a bullet pass from Chandler exploded in Spear's arms. For a split second it seemed as if he caught it, but the ball, apparently too hot to handle, bounced out of his hands.

The ball was returned to the forty-yard line, fourth and five, and Frank Chandler barked, "Punt formation." Moose Moore dropped back and got off a long spiral. Bob Spear, charging downfield to cover the kick, was selected by the Colorado blockers as the key man to stop. One bounced off him, but the second knocked him into a vulnerable position, and a third crumpled him. When the whistle blew, Spear had trouble getting to his feet. His right knee was wrenched; he could not rest his weight on it. Spear was helped off the field, and in at left end went Joe Mandel. Neal Davis moved one notch nearer to the game.

Joe Mandel was on the spot. Colorado immediately aimed their plays at the new Falcon left end. Mandel fought back and gave ground grudgingly, but the constant pounding in the third and fourth quarters took a lot out of him. In the final few minutes of the game he was obviously slow getting downfield under a punt.

The Colorado quarterback took advantage of the opening on his right side. The runback was long, and when the ball carrier was finally stopped at mid-field by Moose Moore, the Falcon coach called, "Davis!"

Neal jumped off the bench. He was nervous, but he was also aware that he was ready—in better shape than he had ever been. He also knew that he was in for it, that Colorado would challenge him immediately. Tensely he welcomed the challenge.

It came in the form of a flying wedge of blockers. They would hit Neal when he was tense and unsure of himself. They would knock him down, wipe him out, and establish a breakthrough in the Air Force defense that could be exploited for the winning touchdown.

Neal was scared for a moment when he saw the flying wedge bearing down on him. In that quick time his body chemistry pumped up adrenaline, and his brain flashed the lightninglike message—flee or fight? There could only be one answer.

He charged. He left his feet. He torpedoed the three members of the flying wedge. They flew this way and that in an explosion of arms and legs. The ball carrier, suddenly confronted by entangling chaos where there had been helpful order, hesitated. Then he turned, cut back, and collided with Moose Moore, who had come up fast.

There was a gain of just half a yard on the play. Second and nine and a half for Colorado on their own thirty-five. They tried the other end and gained two and a half yards, but there were still seven to go for a first down.

Punt formation. Neal was suspicious of it. It was third and seven, to be sure, but there was very little time left to play. It might be a pass off a fake kick. If he charged in fast on the fake, he could easily overrun the passer. Sizing it up this way, he ran in at reduced speed, head up, watching.

The Colorado back caught the ball and shaped it

for a punt. The Air Force right end charged in to block the kick and was suddenly faked off his feet, as the punter became a passer. Neal had held back a little. He knew all the tricks of the ball carrier's trade, the faking and feinting, and he refused to be taken in by any of them. Now he closed in on the passer.

The Colorado back suddenly found himself faced with an alarming choice. He had to get rid of the ball hurriedly or be thrown for a loss. He threw the ball. Considering the pressure, it was a pretty good pass. It was fairly long. It soared over the scrimmage line and then began to lose altitude.

Moose Moore had dropped back for the kick. He moved up when he saw how the play was developing. As a result, he was in a perfect position to intercept the pass. He caught it in the flat on the dead run.

Moose intercepted the pass on the Colorado forty-three-yard line. Before the defenders could put their scattered wits together again, Moose had run the ball back ten yards and was streaking for the goal line.

Only the Colorado back, who had thrown the ball, had a shot at the interceptor. He started to take that shot, but he was suddenly blocked out of the play by the same big end who had hurried the pass. Moose Moore went on all the way for the winning touchdown.

From a recumbent position deep in Colorado territory, Neal watched, strange thoughts turning in his brain. He was exultant over the play and his part in it. He had never before realized how much satisfaction could be derived out of a secondary role in football. Secondary? Yes, secondary. The man who carried the ball was always primary, the first to be noticed, the first to be praised and written up in the papers. The crowd, even the sports writers, rarely noticed who set up the play. They saw only the star who completed it. The wild cheering was for the alert halfback who intercepted the pass and scored the touchdown—not for the end, lying on the ground, who made it all possible.

Yet if Neal wanted to play football for the Falcons this would be his role. But that didn't seem to matter any more. There was a surprising amount of satisfaction in this secondary role, a satisfaction deepened by the acknowledgment of his aid from such players as Moose Moore and Frank Chandler, and some words of praise after the game from the freshman coach.

Here was not the quick take-off of wonderful joy and triumph that faded in a few hours or days. This feeling did not soar to intoxicating heights. Conversely, it did not die as fast. It endured, this feeling of hard-won strength and stamina, gained by a player on trial who has passed the difficult test and knows that he has won himself a chance of playing football on the Falcon varsity.

CHAPTER 14

Falcon football, Neal knew, was named for the famous bird of prey, which was the mascot of the Air Force Academy. Ethan Hoyt was determined to be a falconer. But before he could take up falconry he had to find free time, and this was difficult for any doolie. Grumbling, he took a course called Physical Ed. 100, and he reluctantly admitted that physical conditioning made him feel better and also study better. By finishing his studies more quickly he finally found the free time he needed for falconry.

Neal Davis was humorously skeptical about this sport. Once, just for the fun of it, he remarked, "Falconry—that's for the birds."

Ethan Hoyt failed to see anything funny in this remark. "O.K., wise guy," he said, "come and see for yourself."

"As soon as I can find some free time," Neal replied, using a standard answer. One cold, clear winter day he found the free time.

The captain of the Yankee's team was the chief fal-coner, a first classman named Sperry. Mr. Sperry, wear-ing a gray leather gauntlet, carried one of the trained prairie falcons out of its separate stall in the mews. Neal looked on, still smiling and skeptical. This just couldn't be a sport. Falcons were supposed to be fierce birds of prey. But this brown-and-white bird, perched peacefully on Mr. Sperry's gauntlet, looked as if it would be afraid to start a fight with a sea gull. Why, it even wore a bell on one foot—an ankle bracelet! The falcon was evidently a joke, like most mascots—the Army mule, the Navy goat. Neal smiled tolerantly. He'd go along with the gag, but not much further.

The falcon was still perched peacefully on Mr. Sper-ry's gauntlet as the chief falconer sent Ethan Hoyt trot-ting across the field with a leather lure on a long string. When Sperry released the falcon, the Yankee spun the lure.

Now the skeptical smile on Neal's face faded, for as the falcon took off with powerful grace, it changed its character. No longer did it look like a peaceful pet. It *was* a bird of prey now, with a fierce beak and strong, sharp talons. Quickly gaining altitude, it circled smoothly in the cold, clear air high above the watchers' heads.

Suddenly Mr. Sperry called across the fields, "Bring him down!"

Ethan Hoyt increased the speed of the whirling lure and let it fly.

Spotting the flying lure with its sharp eyes, the falcon zoomed, then dived at almost 200 miles per hour, bell tinkling as it plummeted. Thump. With perfect timing it struck the lure and knocked it to the ground, like a well-trained tackler decisively downing a speeding ball carrier. Then with a few graceful strokes of its strong wings, the bird of prey returned to its master's gauntlet and once again perched there, gracefully, peacefully.

Ethan Hoyt was trotting back across the field, grinning at his roommate. "How'd you like the show?"

Neal grinned back. "You win," he said.

Falconry and football filled what could humorously be called their spare time. Actually there was no such thing at the Academy. Time never dragged. Occasionally it leaped, generally it flew.

"*Tempus*," said the Yankee, using Latin learned at Portland Prep, "*fugit.*"

"I know it flies," said Neal. "Know why? Just take a look at that sked." And he pointed at a schedule of daily duties he had typed up for their mutual guidance.

Reveille	5:55 A.M.
Breakfast formation	6:15
Breakfast and make bed	6:20—7:00

Classes	7:30—11:45
Lunch	1:15—3:10
Sports or Phys. Ed.	3:40—5:10
Dinner	5:45—6:30
Tidy Up	6:30—7:15
Study	7:15—10:15
Taps	10:15

Slowly, however, the roommates managed to learn more about the Academy. They went to the planetarium and were surprised to find that the benches were soft and the backs had headrests. They were not only allowed to lie back and relax; they were invited to do so. "This is a lot better," observed Neal, "than being the Hot Pilot on the dining-room ramp."

The sun was setting in the planetarium while classical music soared beautifully through the stereo system. The afterglow faded, the music swelled, and suddenly overhead stars shone so realistically that the cadets burst their bonds of discipline with cries of wonder and delight. While they watched, the officer in charge of the projector singled out the Big Dipper and, in a matter of seconds, rearranged its stars in a pattern they would form 50,000 years in the future.

There was a special show in the planetarium on Christmas Eve. The projector, run backwards, produced the heavens as they looked the night Christ was born. Fourth classmen Neal Davis and Ethan Hoyt

were not allowed Christmas vacation, a terrible depri-
vation they thought at first. It turned out otherwise.
For one thing all the upperclassmen were gone, and
there were winter sports to enjoy, especially skiing in
the snowbound Rockies.

There came, as always, the slump that follows Christmas holidays. It was, however, a slight slump at the
Academy. The daily schedule left little time for after-
thoughts. The classes at the Academy were kept purposely small, and there was no snoozing in the back
rows.

In one classroom Neal learned how to operate a slip
stick, or slide rule so big that it ran from one wall to
another. Gradually basic math introduced him to
spherical trigonometry and calculus. But the human
side of his education was not neglected. Under an
encouraging instructor named Captain Lubek, Neal
did well in a course called English 101-102, which covered composition, speech, and an introduction to lit-
erature. He also continued with history and foreign
languages.

Neal had come to the Academy expecting a good
deal of flying and studies in astronautics. He was surprised to find that the Academy was more interested
in getting his mind working on why spectacular
achievements in space were possible, and what purpose
they served. The approach seemed to be that any
young man who qualified for this college could master

the gadgets of the jet age. The important thing was to establish for him a frame of reference, a scale of values, by which scientific achievements could be measured according to their real worth to mankind.

The physical and mental sides of the school program were always well balanced. After Christmas vacation Neal took a course called Physical Ed. 101, which covered boxing, judo, and gymnastics, all of which banged him about but increased his strength and agility.

In the spring he turned to tennis and made the freshman team. He was delighted to find that tennis was encouraged at the Academy as a sport that would serve the Air Force officer well for years to come physically and socially.

One year from that fearful day when Neal arrived at the Academy in civilian clothes, he did his last double time in the area. There, standing ramrod straight, he waited for the final inspection by the third classmen.

He did not have long to wait. They were bearing down on him—Cement Face and Corn Pone. But what was going on here? They were smiling. It was a joke, a feint. They would induce a relaxed atmosphere and then smash it with one last abuse of authority. Their tyrannical hands were going up. Ah, at long last they were resorting to physical force—brainwashing having failed, more or less.

But their hands were not raised belligerently. The gestures were conciliatory; the hands were holding insignia, small propellers and wings. The upperclassmen were pinning the insignia on the collars of Neal Davis and Ethan Hoyt and Dell Hubbard. The tyrants were smiling, shaking hands, offering congratulations.

"We knew you'd make it," Corn Pone said.

A miracle, that's what it was.

But Neal still nursed a grudge against them. He still wanted revenge for the humiliations he had suffered at their hands. No smile, no friendly handshake could wipe out those memories. They were too vivid.

Anyway, he was now an upperclassman; he had made it. He was in the end zone, relaxed and triumphant. But wait. Were they moving back the goal posts? Previous experience had taught Neal to be wary of these triumphs.

Yet this one seemed to have remarkable endurance. There were interesting field trips, a tour of Air Force bases, and several flights in the T-29 navigation trainer, known as "the flying classroom." So far so good. Even better was a month's leave at home. Neal basked in the warmth of the family welcome. He could sleep as late as he wished, loaf and lounge in the California sun. He looked up his old friend Billy O'Dell, who greeted him with joy and open admiration. He called on Coach Grigsby and received congratulations. It was all fine—for a while.

But then what Neal had taught himself and what he had learned made even this kind of loafing a bore. His old job as a lifeguard no longer appealed to him. He got work with a road-repair crew, using a pick and shovel, for he knew that as certain as September followed August, autumn meant football—varsity football.

This time the goal posts had been moved back so quietly that he had been unaware of it. The fact sneaked up on him, then smacked him in the face— he was going out for varsity, not for freshman football. He would have to go through the whole painful process of screening and selection all over again. He would have to fight like a Falcon just to survive the squad cut.

It was the old familiar battle, but this time the competition was tougher. Ranked ahead of him at left end were two varsity regulars, Jim Sheridan and Pete Bobko. Up from the freshman team with him would be Bob Spear and Joe Mandel. Suddenly in September, what had seemed almost like a lark, being an upperclassman, became the familiar challenge all over again, as exacting as ever.

Hup-two-kick! Hup-two-bend! The sweat suits gave way to shoulder pads, and the bodies began to fly at the dummies. Hit 'em harder! Only this time they didn't have to say *harder* to Neal. His experience with the Falcon freshmen had sharpened his blocking and tackling. But was it sharp enough for the varsity? Look at the size of this squad! It seemed as if the whole cadet wing had gone out for football. There were not just fifty or seventy-five candidates, there were a hundred players, all working out on this field. Just half of them would survive. And of that number, only four would be left ends.

As the scrimmages began, Neal was not even a member of the four teams that had been formed, but when he was called in to sub for Joe Mandel, he was ready. On defense he was like a knife, cutting and jabbing his way into the third-string backfield. If he failed to make a tackle, he spilled the interference, and made the ball carrier a vulnerable target.

One of the ball carriers had a face that stirred vaguely unpleasant memories. Who was it? Why, it was the old hazer, Cement Face.

When the ball snapped and Cement Face got it, Neal made sure he was in on the play. Jolting a blocker off balance, Neal drove in on the ball carrier, hit him with a good clean tackle, crunched him to the ground, and threw him for a loss.

Scowling, Cement Face surrendered the ball and got to his feet, searching, staring at his adversary, identifying him finally. "Why, it's my old Hot Pilot," he said, in a tone that tried to cover its irritation with a veneer of derision.

"Sorry I spilled your coffee," said Neal with a grin, and then walked away, ending the incident. That was enough. As far as he was concerned the old score was settled. He had learned to distinguish petty issues from big ones. There were many other things more important than personal revenge—making the varsity for one.

This scrimmage now, the day before the cut, was a fiercely contested conflict. Bob Spear was as good as ever, and Joe Mandel was blocking well when his turn came. Then Neal went in at left end for the fourth team.

Punt formation. The fourth team was forced to kick from its own ten-yard line. The third team, leading by one touchdown, was putting on the pressure for another. A good punt runback here might set up a score. Neal knew it as well as any player, and better than most. He had returned many a punt for a good long gain. Time after time his experience as a back had helped him as an end, for he could usually guess what was going on in the ball carrier's mind.

The runback of a punt could be one of the most thrilling plays in football. Now Neal was on the other end of it, the unglamorous defensive end. Never mind, he told himself. Try and make the runback as exciting to the defense as it is to the offense.

The sound of the punt was as thrilling as ever, the starter's gun in a sprint. Go! One quick glance up. There it is—the ball, spiraling downfield, slanting to the left! Slant too, and watch that blocker barreling at you. Use your hands on him and sidestep at the same time. Crunch. You could feel that jolt in both wrists. Forget it; you're still on your feet. Now you're in full stride again, with more room in which to outmaneuver the next blocker. Pretend you're the ball carrier, and he, the tackler. Fake him off his feet. Feint to the right, cut to the left. He's lunging, missing. You needed only one good wrist to deflect that block. (But that left wrist is much stronger than it was at Fairview High.)

Now you've got your prey in the open. Just five yards separate you from the safety man, catching the ball on the bounce. He has timed his catch nicely, so that he doesn't have to break stride.

Now, if you were he, what would you do next? You'd fake toward the side lines and cut back toward the center, trusting that the onrushing end's momentum would carry him headlong past his target.

Anticipating this maneuver, Neal slowed his speed and refused to follow the feint. The safety man swerved, cut back, and collided head on with the end. Crump. The sound was solid and extremely satisfying, in spite of the shock.

Something else was even more satisfying. The force of the collision popped the ball out of the safety man's grip—fumble! The ball dropped, bounced, rolled. A teammate of Neal's, running up, dived for the free ball. Fumble recovered!

When the whistle blew, the fourth team, instead of digging in on defense, found itself in possession of the ball at mid-field. Inspired, it rallied, and drove toward the third-team goal. It was well on its way when the whistle blew, ending the scrimmage.

On the side lines assistant coaches were watching, consulting, comparing notes. The notes, assembled, were taken later to the head coach, Ralph Fleet—a tall, lean man with a weather-beaten face and dark hair, flecked with gray at the temples. Coach Fleet was supervising the scrimmage between the first and second teams. On these teams the left ends were Jim Sheridan and Pete Bobko. Coach Fleet had already heard about two other left ends up from the freshman team—Bob Spear and Joe Mandel. Now he heard about another one, Neal Davis.

Five candidates, but only four would survive the cut. What about this Davis? He was big, but fast for his size. He was shifty, too, something he had apparently learned as a back on his high-school team. It was an attribute for an end. It kept him on his feet when they tried to wipe him out; it got him all the way downfield under punts.

Let's see now. Sheridan and Bobko, veterans; Spear and Mandel, rookies. Spear was strong and consistent, not spectacular but steady. Mandel was all right too, and up to now he had been a little better than Davis in his blocking. But he wasn't as big as Davis or as fast on his feet. Spear was the best blocker of the three rookies. Their tackling was about equal, with Davis apparently developing a natural ability to zero in on the ball carrier.

Five candidates and only four places. Two veterans, three rookies. One of the rookies would have to be dropped.

It was Joe Mandel who broke the news to Neal when the list went up. "Well," said Joe, with a rueful grin, "I made it."

A sharp pang of disappointment stabbed Neal. If Joe had made it, he, Neal, had failed. It was a hard blow, but Neal knew that he would have to hide his feelings, shake Joe's hand, and congratulate him.

Then Joe qualified his statement. "I made the junior varsity," he added.

The junior varsity? This meant then that Joe hadn't made the big team. And if he hadn't—

The picture was completely reversed; Joe was shaking Neal's hand. "Congratulations," he was saying.

The joy of this moment was slightly shaded by shame, as Neal remembered his reaction to Joe's announcement. Instead of immediately being glad for his rival he had been sorry for himself. He would have to get over emotional reactions like that, just as he had cleared other hurdles, athletic and academic.

He was uneasy about something else. The unfortunate part of success in such a highly competitive field

was that it had to hurt one player while helping another. And the player who just missed was the one
who suffered most of all.

Joe Mandel tried to hide his hurt with a grin. "I
guess I've had it," he said.

"Are you quitting?" Neal almost asked, before he remembered how galling the word *quit* had once been
to him.

"I think I'll try out for lacrosse," Joe was saying.
"They tell me it's rough and fast like football."

"I'm sure it is," said Neal. "But aren't you forget-
ting something?"

"What?" said Joe skeptically.

"Chance," said Neal. "Fate, luck, the breaks—the
fumble. The intercepted pass."

Joe frowned. "I don't get it."

"There are four varsity ends," said Neal. "Right?"

"Right."

"Well," said Neal with a grin, "I'm not wishing any
of us bad luck, but any one of us might get knocked
off the A squad by an injury on the field or a flunked
exam in the classroom. There's your break, Joe. If
you're ready for it, you move in. If you're playing
lacrosse, you're out."

Joe continued to frown. "In other words?"

"In other words," said Neal, "why not drop down
and play on the B squad and wait for that break? What
have you got to lose? Just a little prestige."

"Uh-huh," said Joe, still frowning. He thought it over for a minute, and then the frown faded, and he smiled and said, "Neal, I think you've got something."

Neal was somewhat surprised at the success of his argument, but he was pleased. If a cadet was down-hearted, certain encouragement, properly given, could restore his spirit. Probably every cadet at the Academy had sufficient courage and perseverance. But there were still times when it took the right leadership to keep those fires burning.

Leadership. The Academy encouraged it. But Neal was still fairly sure that he wasn't ready for it. He was having a hard enough time holding his own.

CHAPTER 15

Neal warmed the bench when the Falcons beat Trinity and Idaho early in October. These victories were home games, leading up to a road trip which would take the Falcons by plane to Los Angeles, where they would play UCLA. Then they would go all the way from the west coast to the east coast to West Point, where they would play the big one against Army.

Two days before the squad was to take off for Los Angeles, another list went up on a bulletin board, a list of those athletes who would have to devote more time to their studies—athletes who were temporarily ineligible. Under B was the name Bobko—Pete Bobko, second-string end on the varsity. Up went Bob Spear to understudy Jim Sheridan. Up moved Neal Davis to third place. And up from the B squad came Joe Mandel.

When the plane bearing the varsity took off for Los Angeles, Joe Mandel, his grin brighter than ever, was on it. So was someone else Neal hadn't expected to see —Ethan Hoyt. The Yankee was now an assistant falconer. Three mascots were being taken to the game. Between halves they would circle over the Coliseum and dive-bomb the leather lures.

The big plane soared over the Sierras, crossed the California desert, and landed at International Airport, Los Angeles. Neal was in southern California again, as a member of the Air Force Academy varsity football team.

The door of the plane opened, and the Los Angeles weather struck the Falcons full in the face. It was hot, humid, smoggy. The contrast with the cool, clear air of Colorado was depressing. The Falcons felt as if someone had suddenly dropped dirty, hot, wet towels over their faces. It was almost suffocating. Their eyes stung. Their uniforms suddenly seemed chokingly tight around their necks. They were glad to exchange them for sweat suits, brought along for the light workout the day before the game. But how could they play in this atmosphere? When they ran, their lungs ached. Anxiously the coaches scanned the weather forecasts. Unfortunately they were the same for Saturday as for Friday—heat and smog. They would just have to get used to it.

There was a temporary respite when they were taken to their hotel in West Los Angeles near UCLA. The air was clearer here, and there was a swimming pool in which they could cool off. There was also a long-distance call for Neal from San Diego. His family had received the tickets he sent them, but they couldn't make the trip up to Los Angeles. His kid sister Karen had her big chance in a school play, and his father was in Phoenix, Arizona, on a business trip.

Neal was disappointed. But then he looked at it from another angle. The drive up and back to Los Angeles from San Diego would be long, hot, and tiring in the heavy Saturday traffic. And for what? He would probably spend most of the game, if not all of it, on the bench. Sitting in the heat and smog watching twenty-two strangers play football would not be too entertaining for a family that was not athletically inclined.

The smog and the heat still adulterated the air when the Falcons returned to the Coliseum. The Bruins of UCLA were used to it, more or less, but the Falcons found themselves out of their element. Strong ends like Jim Sheridan, who could normally play three full periods out of four, lost a great deal of their zip. Consequently Coach Fleet had to call up one of his rookies, Bob Spear. Spear was a sound player. He did not do anything spectacular, but he was a good steady sub for Sheridan, giving the first stringer much-needed rests from time to time.

Then in the third period Spear, spilling the UCLA interference as they tried to sweep his end, stumbled, turned his ankle, and fell on it hard. When he hobbled out of the game the score stood, Falcons 14, UCLA 13. Rested, Jim Sheridan went back in. But there was a period and a half still to be played.

Jim Sheridan was a first-class end, who hit equally hard on offense or defense. Normally his play was well above average, but now, in the heat and smog, he began to slow down. His blocking lacked its customary crispness, and his tackles, which usually clipped the ball carrier just above the knees, began to hit their target around the hips and sometimes around the shoulders.

For a while Sheridan managed to cover up his declining efficiency, but eventually the UCLA quarterback caught on and began to aim more plays around his right end. Sheridan began to give ground. He gave it up grudgingly, but he gave it up just the same.

The game was in the fourth quarter now, and Coach Fleet was up off the bench, pacing the side lines like a baseball manager watching a weakening pitcher. Should he take Sheridan out or let him go the route? It was a decision that only the coach could make, but he was being helped in it by reports telephoned in by his spotter, watching the play with field glasses high up in the Coliseum.

Coach Fleet had started the game in a state of comparative calm. He liked neither the heat nor the smog, but he knew that there was nothing he could do about the weather and that there was no use worrying about it. He regretted that he had worn a woolen sport jacket and gray flannels—he should have come, he thought, in a seersucker suit. He knew, however, that he was lightly dressed compared to his players in jerseys, shoulder pads, and padded pants. They were the men he felt sorry for.

But as the game progressed, the coach's tension increased, while the players' tension, worked out through exercise, diminished. In the first part of the game Coach Fleet had been able to watch from the bench, getting to his feet only when the Falcons scored their touchdowns. Now in the fourth and final quarter he found it hard to stay still. His sport coat was beginning to feel like a straight jacket; his tie was becoming a noose around his neck. He couldn't seem to get his breath. He longed for the cool, clear air of Colorado. He also longed for his second-string left end, Pete Bobko. Why did he have to flunk his courses at this time of the year? Well, no use worrying about Bobko; he was out of it. Third stringer Bob Spear had done all right until he sprained his ankle. That was a bad break. It put all the pressure on Jim Sheridan, who was obviously tiring. Sooner or later one of the rookies, Davis or Mandel, would have to sub for Sheridan. Coach Fleet feared that moment. This was neither the time nor the place for a rookie.

As the action on the field veered back and forth horizontally, Coach Fleet moved up and down vertically. He paced the side lines; he tugged at his tie; he buttoned and unbuttoned his jacket. He picked up the phone and talked to the spotter, put it down, then picked it up again.

That was a good hole the Falcons had just opened up between the UCLA right guard and tackle. Yes, but on the whistle a new right guard came in for UCLA. And on the next play to the weak side, the Falcon end, Jim Sheridan, missed his block. Hmm.

The Falcons kicked on fourth down. It was a nice punt, a high spiral, but Sheridan was slow getting down under it. His lapse wasn't disastrous, but it aided the UCLA runback by five or maybe ten yards, and every yard gained was valuable at this stage of the game. A fresh end, Coach Fleet knew, would have put that high punt to good use. He would have been right there under it, waiting, when it came down. He might have made the UCLA safety man call for a fair catch, or he could have clobbered him. Either way would have been an improvement on what happened.

The Bruins of UCLA seemed to thrive in this heat and smog. Again Coach Fleet was reminded of a baseball analogy—of those pitchers whose arms warm up in the heat as the game wears on, and who begin to bear down in the late innings. That was what UCLA seemed to be doing right now.

They were aiming a power play around their right end. Jim Sheridan got under it and spilled the interference, but when he got to his feet he was groggy.

Coach Fleet's spotter saw it, but by the time he got the head coach on the phone, Sheridan, still groggy, was mousetrapped on a reverse that went for a full twenty-five yards and put the ball on the Falcon forty. Time out, Air Force.

Coach Fleet hung up the phone and glanced down the bench, his eyes sweeping over the subs. Well, there he was, and he sure was no star; in fact, he was just a rookie. Neal Davis.

He looked big enough certainly. His shoulders were broad, pads or not. He had a good-sized pair of hands, and the muscles on his legs didn't look bunchy like a lineman's, but lean and sinewy—more like a back's. He was undoubtedly in fine shape, but he was probably so tightened up with tension that he couldn't hold a football in either hand. Fortunately he wouldn't have to hold one; he was an end, not a back.

Second by second Head Coach Fleet continued to hesitate. Out on the field Sheridan seemed to revive with a slice of orange and a cup of water. Maybe he could stick it out for a few more plays. But a few more plays like that, and the game would be over, and UCLA the winner.

Sheridan was almost exhausted; Bob Spear was injured. How about Joe Mandel? He hadn't been showing up in the scrimmages as well as Neal Davis. So that was that. There was just one thing to do—gamble on this rookie. In a hoarse voice the head coach said, "Neal Davis."

Having made his decision and summoned his sub, the coach watched to see how the rookie would react, and was slightly startled by what he saw. The rookie popped up like a jumping jack, grabbed his helmet, and came running.

He looked nervous, of course, but he also looked eager and confident as he stood there, strapping his helmet on over his black, short-cropped hair. Coach Fleet wished he could share the rookie's enthusiasm, and hoped he could channel it. This kid was probably as jittery as a cat facing a dog kennel.

Paternally Coach Fleet put his arm around the rookie's shoulder. He had to reach up to do it. This lad was about six foot three, and weighed about 185 pounds. Not bad. He was tense, but he could tackle his way out of his tension. The coach wished he could do the same. The only danger was that this rookie would be too eager. Sometimes it was just as dangerous for an end to go in too fast as too slow. With a gentle pat on the rookie's shoulder, the coach warned his eager beaver. He wished he had more seconds for more warnings, but time was about up out on the field.

"O.K.," was all the coach said now. Not "Good luck" or "God speed," just "O.K." That seemed to sum up everything. There was no need here for a dramatic "Go!" This rookie needed a harness more than a whip.

Coach Fleet had been calm and dignified in the rookie's presence. Now that he was gone, the coach could show his nervousness again. He paced the side lines, sweating, staring. His necktie felt tighter than ever, his sport coat heavier. He was sure that the gray hair on his temples had multiplied and spread all over the sides. He took out his handkerchief and wiped the perspiration off his forehead and his neck. He blinked his smog-stung eyes, closed them, then quickly opened them again. He knew what was coming, a power play, a blitz, aimed right at the rookie, to shock and overwhelm him.

"Hup-two-three." The voice of the UCLA quarterback sounded clear and confident as it made itself audible over the noise of the big shirt-sleeved crowd in the Coliseum.

It was an end run, of course, to the strong side, naturally. Three bruising Bruins from UCLA were bearing down on the rookie. The coach closed his eyes. He felt guilty at having put him in there under all that power and pressure.

The coach couldn't keep his eyes closed for more than a second or so. When he opened them again they widened in hope. The rookie was fighting back, using his hands, his size, his agility. He was going down, but the bruising Bruins were going down with him, all three of them. A Falcon line-backer, coming up fast, was given a clear shot at the ball carrier. He knifed in and cut him down. The gain was exactly one yard. Not bad. Not bad? Good.

The noose around the coach's neck loosened a little. His sport jacket suddenly seemed lighter.

Second and nine. "Hup-two-three." The Bruins faked an end run, tried the middle, and gained two and a half yards. Third and six and a half.

Coach Fleet coughed and mopped his forehead. Third down coming up. Pass probably. That was what the Falcon line-backer was planning for, with his defensive signals. It was an intelligent deployment, but Coach Fleet had a hunch. A pass in this part of the field, at the time of the game, was obvious. A reverse off a fake pass would be smarter. Suck the rookie end in to rush the passer; let him come in all the way and overrun the play. Then turn, toss a lateral, and sweep around the unguarded position left by the absent end.

Coach Fleet's necktie tightened again, and the smog in the air seemed to thicken.

The UCLA quarterback took the ball and faded. The Falcon ends rushed in to hurry the passer. It was one of those times in a coach's career when he wishes it was legal to coach from the side lines, to yell, "Not so fast! Watch that fake!"

Coach Fleet, of course, did no such thing. He simply

stood there tensely and stared, the smog smarting his sweat-blurred eyes. Is that rookie going in too fast, he asked himself, or is it my anxiety that's increasing his speed? The rookie was brushing off one blocker, dodging another. He was nimble for a big guy. His head was up, and he was using his hands well. If he kept that head up and those eyes open, he would be able to see how this play developed.

How was it developing? The Bruin quarterback had the ball cocked for a pass. But the Bruin left half, who had started downfield, had stopped and reversed his field. Suddenly the quarterback pulled the ball down. Simultaneously he side-stepped the Falcon right end, who had charged in too fast.

Fake pass! Coach Fleet groaned. Watch that lateral!

The Bruin quarterback was faking, turning. The Bruin left half was smoothly sweeping back and around. The movements were fluid, precise. One quick thought in the coach's fast-moving mind gave the play grudging admiration before turning again to silent entreaty.

Standing on the side lines, the coach was straining forward. Hands that had clenched came unclenched and rose up, as if reaching for the ball. A deep frown wrinkled the beaded band of perspiration that covered his forehead; a grim expression clamped his mouth shut. Inside he simmered.

Not so the shirt-sleeved crowd in the Coliseum.

They were letting it all out now as they saw the play develop, seeing it twist and turn from a pass to what would be an exciting, wide-open running play, one that would go for a long gain—perhaps all the way.

The Coliseum in Los Angeles had reverted, through tension and excitement and the irritation of the weather, to the atmosphere of the old Roman arena for which it had been named. The sweltering crowd was clamoring for the Bruins of UCLA to devour the Falcons of Colorado. The Bruins were reacting with a nicely executed reverse out of a fake pass, and the crowd was rewarding the effort with a wild roar. Each phase of the play increased the decibels of the din. By the time the Bruin quarterback was ready to toss his lateral, the noise in the Coliseum had swelled to a furious crescendo, an insane symphony of sound.

Without warning, this symphony of sound was pierced by maniacal yips and shrieks, as if some members of the choral group had suddenly snapped their vocal chords. Coach Fleet, ordinarily a gentleman of stern external self-control, was leaping into the air. The band of beaded perspiration on his forehead was tossed, dripping, into the smog by a violent shake of the head. His arms were fully extended, his mouth was open, his frown was gone.

For he had just seen his rookie, that big but agile end, Neal Davis, dart between the Bruin backs and intercept the lateral. The ball gripped tightly in his big right hand, the rookie end was streaking all alone for the UCLA goal line. He was over the Bruin thirty, the twenty, the ten. Touchdown!

Coach Fleet, sorely tempted to try a back flip like a cheerleader, compromised with an Irish jig. As for the crowd in the Coliseum, it was impossible to tell whether they were in favor or against, or just out of their minds.

Coach Fleet had disappeared. Suddenly the Falcon bench had emptied, and all the subs were on the side lines, surrounding the coach, obscuring him. Slowly Mr. Fleet regained his dignity, his face red with heat and happiness. He was sure now, just as sure as he had been that the pass play was a fake, that the game was as good as over. The Falcons, fired up by that spectacular touchdown, might even score another. Plays like this made all the difference in the world to a team, in spirit as well as score. For that matter, a player like this Neal Davis could—

Ah-hmmm. It was an almost silent clearing of the coach's smog-clogged throat, a noise so small that it was just a whisper in a howling wind of screams and shouts. It was small but significant. Coach Fleet, his tension relieved by the spectacular score, was able once again to detach himself from this pandemonium and think ahead. He was still thinking ahead as the Falcons converted for the point after touchdown, and the score became Air Force 21, UCLA 13.

Ah-hmmm. The coach cleared his throat again for good measure as the Falcons kicked off. He was still standing on the side lines, but he wasn't pacing them. His necktie felt much looser, his jacket far lighter. The air seemed to be clearer now. The smog seemed to have thinned out. Could all this comfort and clarity be psychological? Possibly. Strain and stress played strange tricks on the mind.

Coach Fleet was still a little nervous, but it was the low-pitched pleasant excitement that always precedes a kickoff, one of the most wide-open plays in football. There was the solid thump of the ball, the kick, end-over-end, deep. And who was fast down under it? That big rookie, Davis. Coach Fleet began to glow again. The kid was inspired. He was going through the Bruins like a scatback—faking, feinting, zeroing in, charging. Crunch. He was nailing the Bruin ball carrier on the UCLA twenty-five-yard line. Not only had he sharply curtailed the runback, he had pumped new pep into the Air Force team. It was as if some invisible trainer had suddenly slipped every Falcon a canister of pure oxygen. Inhaled, it gave new life to tired lungs.

Head Coach Fleet decided that he could go back to the bench and sit down. Happily he took a call from his spotter.

"Say, Coach, what about that rookie at left end? How *about* that?"

Yes indeed, how about that? Was the spotter trying

to take all the credit for the well-timed substitution? Well, let him. It didn't matter. Something else mattered now. This game was just about over. What mattered now was the big game against Army at West Point on the following Saturday.

It was the Army team, Coach Fleet remembered, that had worked an effective play with what they called the lonesome end. Army's lonesome end took an isolated position far from the huddle. There he was a constant worry to opponents. Was he a pass receiver or just a decoy? It was too late sometimes before the opponents found out.

It would be a fine thing, thought Coach Fleet, to turn the tables on Army—to come up suddenly with a secret weapon involving the very player Army had used—an end. Part of the secret weapon could be this rookie end, Neal Davis. The other part of it might be that promising quarterback who had also come up from the freshmen, Frank Chandler. The two of them might team up for something new and spectacular, a nice surprise to pull on Army next week at West Point.

With these happy thoughts percolating, Coach Fleet sat back on the bench and watched his team play the final minutes of the game against UCLA.

Up in the stands someone else was watching—Major Stone, a member of an Academy faculty group that had come to Los Angeles for the game. Major Stone had white hair, contrasting with a young, ruddy face that was usually decorated with a pipe. Like other members of the Air Force faculty, he was a keen student of leadership. And he had been impressed by what he had seen in the last few minutes. A rookie, who was ready, mentally and physically, had plunged into his first varsity game and by aggressive and skillful play had stopped the enemy advance and had assured victory for the Academy.

Next week, Major Stone was sure, Coach Fleet would make good use of this rookie at Michie Stadium, West Point. But Major Stone was thinking of another exciting field in which the rivals competed. The name of Neal Davis had already been submitted as a possible competitor in this field by a fellow member of the faculty, Captain Lubek.

Captain Lubek had discussed Cadet Davis' potential. Now Major Stone had just seen something of Cadet Davis' potential, and he was impressed. He made a mental note to review the cadet's record. Then, perhaps, he would talk to him about being a candidate for this other competition, which, in his opinion, was equally exciting and even more important.

CHAPTER 16

The object of all these observations was blissfully unaware of them. Neal remained unaware of them as the
Falcons flew back to Colorado. All he needed to know
was that he had made the varsity—made it with a bang.
Nothing else mattered. Why, even members of the
first team—those untouchables—now went out of their
way to speak to him. Gadzooks!

Just a week or so ago he had been a lowly fourth
stringer, barely able to survive the cut. Now he was
right up there with the best of them. Moreover, he had
actually been one of the stars of the game—it said so
in the Los Angeles papers. It was pure joy. It was all
he wanted. This was the nicest end zone he had ever
entered. He could stay here forever.

He stayed there Saturday night and all day Sunday.
There was no scrimmage scheduled for Monday, just a
light workout and a skull session. That would be simple. It was, until Neal was given his special assignment.

The assignment was outlined in a side-line conference with Head Coach Fleet. It was quite different
from their side-line conference in the Coliseum. Coach
Fleet, comfortable in baseball cap and sweat suit, was
calm, almost casual. But his plan was exciting. In the
game against Army, Neal was going to be half of a secret weapon. The other half was Frank Chandler, out
there on the field now throwing bullet passes. The
regular assignments at left end were to be handled by
Jim Sheridan and Bob Spear, whose sprained ankle
had mended. Neal Davis and Frank Chandler were
to be trained for a special performance, and the training would start almost at once.

"Yes, sir," said Neal. What else could he say? To
be selected for a secret assignment was his reward for
his play against UCLA. What did he expect—to lounge
about, luxuriating in the end zone? Of course he
couldn't. They were bound to move back the goal posts.
They always had, hadn't they?

"Hup-two-three." On "three" Frank Chandler took
the ball from center, faked a hand-off to the fullback,
and faded. At the same time Neal ran straight down,
feinted to keep on going that way and then, cutting
into the center slot, buttonhooked. As he turned, the
bullet pass exploded in his hands—or at least it was
supposed to. Sometimes it landed around his knees or
flew over his head. Once it hit him before he had time
to turn. For it was a play in which the timing had to

be split-second perfect, and it wasn't at first. But under the watchful eyes of an assistant coach called Larsen, who drilled the two over and over again, the timing improved, and the percentage of passes completed sharply increased. Monday, Tuesday, Wednesday. When the varsity flew east to New York, Neal Davis and Frank Chandler were working well together.

It was the first time Neal had ever seen the skyscrapers of Manhattan. It was almost impossible to associate this spectacular metropolis with an island, purchased for a pittance from Indians. That made it all the more strange to explore the beautiful but somber reaches of the Hudson River. Here, in some places, time had stood still, and the imagination, looking down from the rock-bound Storm King Highway, could easily piece together a picture in which Benedict Arnold turned traitor or British agent André was captured by card-playing Continentals.

In Los Angeles everything had been bewilderingly bright and garish, as well as sprawling, transient, and hot. At West Point everything was old, traditional, and compact—and grim and cold. The scud, racing across the lowering sky, was gloomily gray. The cold air, dampened by the Hudson, had a penetrating chill. Here were no squealing coeds in bright cotton dresses, but a stern, gray corps of West Point cadets, startling their opponents with the ferocity of their organized shouts, or depressing them with the dirge of their long "Arrrmmmaaay" cheer, a mournful wail that dragged out across the frozen plain and echoed against the rocks over the river.

Neal warmed up with the squad. Two Falcon passers took turns throwing to the backs and ends. One of them was Frank Chandler, but the practice passes he threw to Neal were no different from those thrown to everyone else. The secret weapon was kept secret, they hoped. It was to be sprung as a surprise at a certain time and place.

But when? That was what was worrying Neal now as the game progressed. Both teams scored twice, but in the third period Army bulldozed down the field, and using its lonesome end as a decoy, plunged through the center of the line for a touchdown, which put it ahead by six points, 20-14. On the bench sat Neal Davis and Frank Chandler, watching, waiting, and shivering.

Well into the fourth period the score remained the same. Alternating at left end, Jim Sheridan and Bob Spear were playing hard and well. Joe Mandel had not been needed, and it looked to Neal as if he might not be needed either. There were now only five minutes left to play, and the Falcons still had a fighting chance. Here, on an end run, they seemed to be going somewhere. But an Army line blocker spilled the interference, and an Army defensive back forced the ball carrier out of bounds. The run was long, but it was sideways, not forward. The Falcons then tried a long pass to Bob Spear. It was a beautiful pass, but at the last second the Army safety man leaped up and batted the ball down. The Falcons had failed by five yards to make a first down, and were forced to kick.

On the bench Neal huddled with the rest of the subs, hands crammed in parka pockets, hoods pulled over heads. Suddenly something tapped Neal on the hood. He turned and looked up at Assistant Coach Larsen. Larsen spoke quietly. "Go in on the next whistle," he said.

What about Frank Chandler, the other half of the secret weapon? Neal didn't ask the question, because he had already thought of the answer. If both members of the two-man team went in on the same whistle, the opponents might put two and two together and get their defenses set.

Neal's hands were warm, but the rest of his body was stiff and cold. He warmed it up quickly with a few exercises and a couple of sprints up and down the side lines. Something cold lightly stung his face, then bathed it with a cool drop of water. He jerked his head up, put his hand to his face, and realized that he had been startled by a snowflake. In Los Angeles it had been smog; at West Point it was going to be snow. A cold shiver ran down Neal's spine. How would he ever catch a fast pass in a snowstorm? But the snow that had started to fall soon stopped, and the flurry of flakes swirled off the field like a small white cyclone. It disappeared, but it might still return. The threat hung overhead in those low gray clouds, which menaced like the sword of Damocles. Across the field the gray-clad corps of cadets was wailing the long drawn-out dirge, "Arrrmmmaaay." Mournfully it echoed back from the grim rock-bound hills and suddenly exploded. "FIGHT, TEAM, FIGHT!"

Nervously Neal sucked in his breath and shivered again. The cold, gray setting and the psychological warfare were getting him down. It took a strong effort to put down a growing feeling of panic.

Without warning, the referee's whistle blew—sharp, strident. With an effort Neal pulled himself together. He had to answer that whistle and force himself out on the field, cleats thudding against the frozen turf. Bob Spear passed by on the way out. He trotted off, staring straight ahead, as if he was irked by the substitution. Neal did not feel slighted. It was all part of the plan to make him as inconspicuous as possible. It had to look like a natural progression from the first stringer Jim Sheridan—battered—to Bob Spear—tiring —and so on down naturally, to the third-string end, Neal Davis.

The clock showed four minutes to play. Army had the ball, second and seven on their own thirty-three.

As Neal expected, the West Pointers aimed their first play right at his position. It was his first experience with Army blocking. It blasted him with a force that almost took his breath away. He reeled, staggered, and was thumped down on the frozen field. In Los Angeles he had taken three UCLA blockers down with him; at West Point he took only one. With the Falcon left end flattened, the Army ran for seven yards and a first down.

A noise like a clap of thunder burst from the cadet corps and vibrated unpleasantly in Neal's ears. He got up quickly, more shocked than hurt. Falcon training had brought him through almost unscathed physically, but he was angry mentally. They had run right over him. Not only that, they had made a first down on their own forty. If they kept that up they would score another touchdown, and the game would be gone for good.

Muscles tensed, he tried to dig in, like a soldier chopping a foxhole out of a frozen battlefield. The ground refused to give way. He dug in mentally instead. He hoped they would try the same play again. This time he would be ready for them.

It was almost the same play. This time the ball carrier started wide, as if on a sweep, then cut back inside the end and the tackle. Two Army blockers came at Neal. He dodged one, manhandled the other, and found himself face to face with the ball carrier. Lunging forward, Neal went in low. He hit the ball carrier just above the knees and thumped him down hard.

The cadet corps rumbled its disapproval. The gain was one yard. Second and nine. That was better, Neal thought. Still, Army had gained eight yards through his position in just two plays. That was eight yards too much. Indignantly he kicked his cleats against the frozen turf. He had been sure that Army would aim their first two plays at him. He wasn't so sure about the third play. He tried to put himself in the Army quarterback's place and do his thinking for him. That rookie at left end for Air Force. We flattened him for a seven-yard gain, but then he bounced back. He might be overeager now. Let's let him in, mousetrap him, and swing a deep reverse around him.

When the ball snapped, there was an opening, and Neal knifed in. Then he slowed down, suspicious. This was too good to be true. Out of the corners of his eyes he saw the Army left half suddenly turn and scuttle sideways—mousetrap.

Neal's head and hands were up. Even so, the block was so hard it staggered him. But he recovered his balance in time to see the quarterback fake a hand-off to the right half and give the ball to Army's left end, who had swung back. Reverse. His analysis had been right. He had not been duped.

The Army end was racing wide, and Neal was chasing him. Trapped, the ball carrier tried to cut back. He skidded, and Neal skidded with him. At the same time, reaching out with his right arm, Neal grabbed and held on, and they went down together in a thumping tangle. It was not a clean classical tackle, but it was an effective one, for it meant a five-yard loss to Army. The thunder of the cadet corps crackled its dismay. It was third down and fourteen to go.

Army went into punt formation. Neal charged in, eager to block the kick. *He* was blocked instead, with a holding block that stuck to him like flypaper. The Army kicker took one step forward. Whump. He got off a good long punt.

Neal had failed to block the kick. He was irked by his failure, until he remembered that he was playing for a football team that should not let slight setbacks affect it.

The punt had carried about fifty yards, many of them in Falcon territory. The Army ends, fast down the frozen field, held the runback to ten yards. It was first and ten, Air Force, on its own thirty-five-yard line. Into the game at quarterback, as if it were just an ordinary substitution, came Frank Chandler.

Frank glanced at the clock. So did Neal. There were now two minutes and forty-five seconds left to play. What were Frank's instructions? Would he use the buttonhook pass immediately?

Apparently not. He was calling running plays up

the middle and off the tackles. Conservative football. We won't win this way, thought Neal. But he obediently carried out his blocking assignments.

Third and four. "Punt formation!" barked Frank Chandler.

"Block that kick!" roared the corps of cadets.

It was a fake kick. Frank dropped back ten yards behind center and passed directly to the Falcon fullback, who rammed up the middle. He missed the first down by a yard.

Fourth and one on the Falcon forty-four. Suddenly the crisis had come to its climax. If the Falcons tried and failed on the fourth down, Army would get the ball in Air Force territory. If the Falcons kicked, Army had the ball in their own territory, where they would probably freeze it for the rest of the fleeting time.

In the huddle all eyes were on Frank Chandler. His voice was hoarse with tension as he spoke the words Neal had been waiting for, "Buttonhook on three."

This was it! An emotional wave, built up by the long wait, suddenly struck Neal, almost washing away his mental defenses, to let fear flood in. Feverishly his brain leaped from one thought to the next. He had expected a punt or a line plunge. But Frank Chandler, who had seemed so conservative, was now making the biggest gamble of all. Why?

The Falcon backfield was going into a formation that seemed to promise a running play, a quick plunge for the one yard that was needed. Accordingly, Army was massing its men up front with a seven-man line and two line-backers, all arrayed to stop the frontal assault. That left only two backs on the far end of the defensive box and a big hole in the center slot, just where Frank Chandler wanted it.

Neal's thoughts were flicking by in seconds—sticky, sweaty, stomach-stirring seconds.

"Hup!" Chandler's voice was hoarse, harsh. It grated on Neal's ears. You're putting me on the spot, he protested silently.

"Two!" Neal swallowed his protest with a gulp. On "three" it would be for better or worse, all or nothing. He would fake and feint in the Army backfield, while Frank Chandler did the same in his own.

Neal simulated the role of an end, anxious to carry out an important blocking assignment. He had no difficulty acting anxious. Tension was playing strange tricks on him. He moved an arm or leg without realizing it. He saw, but he did not see.

"Three!" Go! He tensed forward, brush blocked the Army end, and feinted, as if to throw a block on the Army line-backer. Then he ran downfield, cut, and buttonhooked in the center slot. He turned, opened his eyes physically as well as mentally, and faced stark reality.

What he saw alarmed him. Frank Chandler had drawn in the Army defenders with his fake plunge, but his bullet pass had been thrown too high, too horribly high. It was going over Neal's head!

He jumped. His long arms, his big hands, stretched every tendon. Smack. The ball hit his fingers with a wonderful stinging pain. He had stopped the flight of the errant pass.

Then he dropped it!

It had been too fast. He couldn't hold on to it. Escaping from his fingers, it bobbled toward the ground. Desperately he stabbed at it again. Frantically his fingers touched it, clutched it. His acrobatics made him stumble and skid, but somehow he stayed on his feet.

Quickly he came into the clear, like a diver, who, almost suffocated, struggles up and bursts to the bright and shiny surface. Suddenly, spectacularly, he had become what he had always longed to be, a ball carrier in a broken field—and not just an ordinary field. It was the frozen ground at Michie Stadium, West Point, in the big game against Army.

He was running across the fifty-yard line before the surprised defenders could start closing in on him, one from the right, the other from the left. Surprised at first, they were now grim and determined. They wanted revenge for the trick he and Frank Chandler had played on them. They wanted to trap this upstart, hit him so hard that the ball would be jarred loose, the fumble recovered, the scoring threat ended, and the Army victory assured.

Two against one. But Neal happened to be in his element. He had carried out the nerve-racking part of his assignment, catching that high bullet pass. He was beginning to enjoy this phase of the play. Running at three-quarter speed, he planned his move, then made it. Feinting to the right, he faked a dash to the side lines. Suddenly he cut back. The Army defender on the right turned, skidded, lunged—and missed.

One down, one to go. The maneuver had eliminated one enemy, but it gave the other a good shot at the target. He fired.

Neal was ready. His defense was a jolting straight-arm from a wrist that had been persistently strengthened for just such an occasion. The straight-arm landed squarely on the enemy helmet. It jolted the enemy head just enough to spoil the timing of the tackle. The full tackle became a half tackle, one arm around one leg. Without losing his balance, Neal spun in a 360-degree turn that twisted him free and put him completely in the clear.

He went all out now, heart pounding, cleats pounding, the cold, damp wind singing beautifully in his ears. The goal line, the end zone—touchdown, triumph, glory!

Teammates were running up, whacking him on the back, leaping into the air. A flurry of snowflakes, swirling down from low-flying clouds, fell on him like a handful of confetti. The grim grayness of West Point suddenly acquired a friendly glow. Frank Chandler, swept up in the exciting spirit of sudden victory, switched signals on the conversion, faked a kick, and fired a better bullet pass straight into Neal's arms for two points after touchdown. The game came to a close with Neal again in the end zone, triumphant. It seemed at the time like a wonderfully permanent position.

CHAPTER 17

Neal's exultant feeling persisted in the minutes, hours, days, and weeks that followed the game at West Point. In the concluding games on the Falcon schedule the new combination of Frank Chandler, passer, and Neal Davis, receiver, worked havoc among Air Force opponents—going for short gains, long gains, touchdowns. And when it didn't go, it was such an effective decoy that other Falcon offensives gained greatly in surprise and strength.

In the end of his sophomore season Neal was a full-fledged Falcon. He could look forward to being, in his junior year, the first-string left end. It was not beyond the realm of possibility that he would become captain-elect of the team at the end of his junior season.

What more could he want? Nothing. The rest of his life at the Academy was a fitting complement to his successful athletic career. His grades were good, especially in history and English. He was doing some writing for the Academy magazine, the *Talon*. His experience with gliders near San Diego had steered him into becoming a member of the Soaring Club. In the spring he would probably become number-two man on the varsity tennis team. Come summer, he might exercise his right to swap his leave for an airplane tour, all expenses paid, of Air Force bases in Europe.

As the saying goes, he had it made.

But there was one person who disagreed with Cadet Neal Davis—faculty member Major Stone. One cold, clear winter day the major called Cadet Davis in for a conference.

Neal wondered what it was all about. He knew he would be taking Stone's political-science course in his junior year. He had seen the major on campus, and remembered him as an officer with a ruddy complexion and white hair, who smoked a pipe. But why was Major Stone calling him in now?

The major put down his pipe, smiled in friendly fashion, and shuffled a neat stack of papers. Previous experience indicated to Neal that the stack of papers probably concerned his personal history. Once upon a time in high school this might have been cause for concern. No longer. He was in fine shape, academically and athletically. He had earned this end zone, and he was going to stay in it. If Major Stone, on reviewing Neal's record, came to the conclusion that Cadet Davis should volunteer to become an astronaut, the major was mistaken.

But Stone wasn't talking about astronauts; he was talking about Rhodes scholars, students who won scholarships to Oxford University in England.

This vaguely rang a bell in Neal's memory. Where? When? Oh yes, Cadet Gregson—his tour of Europe. He had met an Academy graduate who had won a Rhodes scholarship.

Major Stone went on talking. He had a quiet, friendly voice. Nice office too, fine furniture. Picture window, naturally. Nice view. Plenty of snow on the mountains. Good skiing this week end.

What was Major Stone saying? That Rhodes scholars couldn't just be eggheads. Cecil Rhodes, founder of the famous project, had stipulated that his fund sponsor students whose intellectualism was combined with participation in sports.

Good idea, thought Neal.

Major Stone was glancing at one of the papers on his desk. "I see you play tennis as well as football, Mr. Davis."

"Yes, sir."

The major smiled in his casually friendly way. "Tennis has a good standing at Oxford, too. As a matter of fact, Mr. Davis, the competition for Rhodes scholarships is something like a major tennis tournament. There are qualifying rounds, in which the colleges select their candidates. If you win your college round, you proceed to the next one—the State Selection

Board. Win this round, and you go on up—say, to the semifinals, the regional round. There are eight regions in the United States. Each region has four scholarships. This is the final round. Win here, and you get the big prize."

"Sounds like quite a tournament, sir," said Neal. He was interested—slightly.

"It is," said Major Stone. "In the entire United States there are only thirty-two winners annually. Every winner receives $2000 for each school year at one of the world's greatest universities." Major Stone smiled. "As tournaments go, Mr. Davis, I'd say that this was one of the best."

One of the best, thought Neal. Imagine that now. Hmm. That tournament analogy was pretty good. Qualifying for the Academy had been like winning a tournament. And he had won that when, comparatively at least, he was in questionable shape, physically and mentally. He should have a better chance of winning this one, which Major Stone called one of the best. That would be something.

Major Stone's pipe had gone out. He was emptying it into an ash tray and scraping the bowl with a penknife. There was something about this pipe business, Neal thought, that was fascinating and sort of soothing at the same time, like a snake charmer's flute.

"I notice," said Major Stone, tapping his pipe against the ash tray, "that you do well in English and history, Mr. Davis. I see, too, that you have been doing some writing for the *Talon*."

"Yes, sir," said Neal. It was pleasant to have these things noticed. He felt that he and Major Stone were already friends.

The major was now filling his pipe from a tobacco pouch, an interesting procedure—dip-pack, dip-pack. "Extracurricular writing," said the major, "is the sort of thing that helps in this Rhodes tournament. It's like having a superior stroke in tennis, a sharper volley or a faster serve."

"Yes, sir," said Neal. He was beginning to feel right at home here—more at home, in fact, than he felt at home. Strange, wasn't it? Moreover, he was beginning to be rather interested in this tournament. After all, it was flattering to be called in and considered as a candidate. And Major Stone was so casual; there was nothing high-pressure here at all.

The pipe was packed. Deliberately, the major lit it, drew on it. A small cloud of blue smoke drifted across the desk. It had a sweet, good smell. The major, pulling peacefully on his pipe, was now talking about West Point—about how gratifying it was to beat Army at anything, because West Pointers were such good competitors.

Neal agreed. He was proud of his contribution to that football victory over West Point. It was still, after all this time, a satisfying feeling.

But the major was speaking of victories in other fields. Apparently West Point had won an astonishing number of Rhodes scholarships.

"Is that so, sir?" said Neal. Think of that now. Hmm. Well, if West Pointers could do it, so could Falcons. Couldn't they?

Major Stone was answering the unasked question. "We're pretty far behind," he admitted. "But don't forget that we've just begun to fight. Remember, Mr. Davis, we didn't graduate a class until 1959. Yet in that very first year we won a Rhodes scholarship."

Good, thought Neal. He liked the way Major Stone included him with "we." "We" of the Air Force Academy. It was a proud feeling. But it made him feel all the more disturbed that West Point should be so far ahead in international scholarship.

"One of the most famous Rhodes scholars from West Point," Major Stone continued, "was a man you may remember—Pete Dawkins, the football star. He played Rugby for Oxford."

Rugby. Neal pricked up his ears even higher. He had never played Rugby, but if it was good enough for Pete Dawkins—

Major Stone, it developed, had played some Rugby while stationed in England with the Air Force. "It's a good deal like football," he was saying, "but it moves faster. It's a wide-open game."

"Sounds great, sir," said Neal. He was now very much interested.

Major Stone smoked and smiled. "Some of our young people think that English athletes are slightly on the sissy side, because they play cricket. They should try Rugby. It's just as rough as football. You don't wear pads in your pants or on your shoulders. You play in shorts and an unpadded jersey. If you're injured you keep on playing, if you can, because no substitutes are allowed."

"I see, sir," said Neal. He saw indeed, and he liked what he saw.

"In my opinion," said Major Stone, "Rugby would be an ideal game for a player of your size and experience, Mr. Davis. The play of an end in football is very much like the play of a back in Rugby. The same situations come up, the need for crisp tackling, good ball carrying, and the catching of quick passes. It should fit you to a T, Mr. Davis."

T as in T formation, thought Neal, tea as served daily in England. It sounded fine. Playing Rugby for Oxford, he would be a back again. By that time, if he won the tournament, he would have earned the privilege.

When the talk with Major Stone ended, Neal left on a wave of enthusiasm. But when the force of the wave died out, he was left high and dry on a beach of second thoughts and skepticism. He had the uneasy feeling that he had fallen hook, line, and sinker for another challenge.

To be sure, Major Stone did not use the technique of Coach Grigsby or Cadet Gregson. As a matter of fact, the new challenge had been presented so casually, so calmly, so quietly, that it hardly seemed like a challenge at all. It was more of a compliment. He had been called in and informed that he could consider himself—if he wanted to—a candidate in this great tournament. There was no implication whatsoever that he would flop. On the contrary, he had been encouraged all along the line. This was no challenge; it was simply an invitation to a new and exciting career in the international field.

However, a small voice continued to send warnings. Beware of this ambitious scheme. Was Major Stone's talk a soft sell? It might hide a hard core that would crack you over your knuckles, if not your noggin. You're in the end zone right now—you've earned it— and it's very comfortable. You are beginning to be rather popular; you have won prestige; you may be elected captain of the Falcon football team. What more do you want? Stay in this end zone. Don't let them move the goal posts back again. That's what Major Stone is doing, you know.

Time flew by, Falcon time, every minute full. There

were new courses to take, secondary sports, the Soaring Club, extracurricular writing.

Now there was the question of what to do with the thirty-day summer leave—whether to take it or go on a tour of Europe. Neal decided to take the tour. So did falconer Ethan Hoyt, Joe Mandel, Dell Hubbard, and Frank Chandler.

In London, England, they met an Academy graduate named Eric Bolton, a Rhodes scholar, who was spending his summer as an assistant to the Air Attaché of the American Embassy. Bolton was pleasant but reserved, as if he had already assimilated an English characteristic. Yet he was polite and obliging to the students from his alma mater. He arranged a week end at Oxford for them.

The sun happened to be shining. The spires of the chapels and churches rose gracefully over the narrow streets. The beautiful old buildings of the University reflected a soft light, enhanced by the deep green of the grass, the rich leaves of the old trees. Nothing could have been more different physically from the setting of the Air Force Academy. It was evident that Oxford was completely different, too, in other ways. There was no statement by Rhodes scholar Bolton, saying that this system was superior. But there was a definite implication that this system certainly had its merits and was an experience that a qualified student should not miss.

The cadets borrowed equipment and played tennis on grass courts. They rowed and swam in the river. They inspected the field where Rugby was played. They climbed a medieval staircase and had tea and sandwiches in Bolton's rooms. Slowly, imperceptibly, the beauty and traditions of the place, and all they stood for in the minds of men, sank in.

Looking back on it, Neal could remember only one thing Eric Bolton said that could in any way have been construed as a challenge. "You're pretty much on your own here," he had said. "It's quite a change after the Academy."

It would be, Neal agreed. Quite a change, quite a challenge. He kept turning this thought over in his mind as they returned to London. It stayed with him as they flew back to the United States. It was night, and the big jet was flying smoothly at high speed far above the Atlantic Ocean. Inside the plane it was dim, hushed—a perfect place for meditation. Here for a few hours you were detached from the restless world. It was ironical that the interior of a jet, a plane that had radically quickened the pace of living, could offer a kind of suspended sanctuary under the stars. Calmly, you could think back over the last frantic few years, to your B or B-plus high-school days. You could thank your lucky stars—some of them seemingly so close— for the challenge that had spurred you on and up. How many others in the B group could have responded if challenged—if pushed, pulled, or inspired? Some—perhaps many.

The Air Force Academy pushed you and pulled you and inspired you. With its help and with a considerable effort of your own, you reached a highly satisfactory end zone. And you could stay there if you felt like it. You could ignore Major Stone and Rhodes scholar Eric Bolton, who were moving back the goal posts. You could ignore their talk about your qualifications and West Point's fine record and Rugby and the difficulty of being on your own in a great university after four years of stern discipline. You could ignore them if you felt like it. But, after all that you had done, did you feel like it?

In the fall of his third year at the Academy Neal took a course called Political Science 202 under Major Stone. It was after one of these classes that Neal approached the associate professor and said, "Major, I've decided to try for that Rhodes scholarship."

Major Stone smiled. "I thought you would," he said.